AND TO SAY HELLO
SHORT STORIES

SCOTT RANDALL

AND TO SAY HELLO
SHORT STORIES

LIVRES
DC
BOOKS

Cover illustration by Manon Gauthier.
Author photograph courtesy of the author.
Book designed and typeset by Primeau Barey, Montreal.

Library and Archives Canada Cataloguing in Publication
Randall, Scott, 1970- , author
And to say hello: short stories/Scott Randall.
ISBN 978-1-927599-29-7 (bound).
ISBN 978-1-927599-28-0 (pbk.)
I. Title.
PS8585.A5454A63 2014   C813'.54   C2014-906999-5

For our publishing activities, DC Books gratefully acknowledges the financial
support of the Canada Council for the Arts, of SODEC, and of the Government
of Canada through Canadian Heritage and the Canada Book Fund.

Canada Council   Conseil des Arts
for the Arts   du Canada

Société
de développement
des entreprises
culturelles
Québec

Printed and bound in Canada.
Interior pages printed on FSC® certified environmentally responsible paper.
Distributed by Fitzhenry and Whiteside.

FSC
www.fsc.org
MIX
Paper from
responsible sources
FSC® C095263

DC Books
PO Box 666, Station Saint-Laurent
Montreal, Quebec H4L 4V9
www.dcbooks.ca

For Sharon and Alen

CONTENTS

LANEY WILSON AND WAITING

Forty-five minutes into his rowing machine routine, Father imagines Samantha and Laney Wilson living in Montreal. They're in school, but since neither his daughter nor her friend can afford fulltime tuition, they've been working retail and taking a night course whenever they can. Ambitious young women, they're no more than one or two credits shy of their degrees by now. Laney in Microbiology and his daughter Samantha in something slightly less arduous. Sociology maybe. Their apartment is a one-bedroom, advertised as a three-room in that odd Montreal way. Samantha has set up her belongings in the living room, her IKEA bed and a curbside-salvage desk pushed up against a ceiling-high window. On clear mornings, she can just make out Mt Royal Park from bed, and in the summer, the two of them walk up and jog down the mountain path three evenings a week. The routine is Laney's idea, good for physical fitness and good for an inexpensive night out of the house. Laney looks out for Samantha like that, makes sure both of them get a healthy amount of exercise.

Father thinks *deaf-mute francophone* (38 results found). He pushes hard against the rowing machine footrests, strengthening his quick backward stroke and stretching himself out fully. The plastic of the left footrest snaps at the arch of his foot, and he stops.

He bought his first treadmill some eighteen months ago, just after the trial separation began. Most of the family room furniture went with Karen, leaving the once-crowded townhouse basement empty but for the television. The first treadmill was a CardioTrac 2000, a $150 purchase on usedottawa.com. The previous owner drove a truck and agreed to deliver for an extra twenty.

At first, Father eased into his exercise routine. His weight had never been more than ten or fifteen pounds over what it should be, but it'd been that way for decades. When he thought about it, his clothes hadn't really fit comfortably since university–not since before work, before Karen, before Samantha. After so many inactive years, easing into an exercise routine made sense. Set up in front of the television, he programmed the treadmill for a brisk walking pace–no more than three miles an hour–and exercised his way through whatever thirty-minute sitcom happened to come on. This after-dinner routine lasted every day for two weeks, at which time, he sped up to a slow four-mile-an-hour jog and an hour-long drama. Usually a medical or legal programme. He tried police procedurals a few times, but they all seemed to be about putting sweet-faced children in abusive and dangerous situations.

His breathing was a pant on the treadmill, but alone in the emptied house, he could turn the television volume up and drown out the sound.

He sits waiting for the light at his least favourite intersection in Ottawa. Greenbank and Fallowfield. Here, two lanes reduce to one just north of the lights. It's the suburbs, and no one driving this route at seven thirty in the morning hasn't been here a hundred times before. And yet, every Monday to Friday, Father watches as commuter after commuter switches to the right-hand lane at the last minute. The lights change, the cars floor their accelerators, and on the other side of the intersection, traffic congests into a bottle-neck. Aggression and selfishness, such is human nature.

While he waits, he notices a faded decal on the rusting trunk of the Ford Tempo ahead of him. It's peeling and near-disintegrated from years of city road salt, but the CN Tower logo is still dis-cernible, and Father imagines Samantha and Laney Wilson living in Toronto. They've been there for over a year now, and one idle Sunday noon after their daily hour at the gym, Laney suggests they visit the CN Tower. Monday at the office is eighteen short hours away, and Laney wants to do something different. Samantha complains that it's too touristy and a waste of money. She wants to go back to the apartment and flake with a paperback, but Laney glares. They went to that Club Heptagon opening thing a week ago and she didn't really didn't want to do that either. Samantha concedes, and the afternoon turns out wonderful. After the observation deck, they eat an overpriced apple torte in the 360 Restaurant and decide to pay the extra money for the Sky Pod, where they borrow a pair of binoculars from a flirty tourist visiting the city by himself. Scanning the tops of the buildings, Samantha locates their apartment building, and when it's Laney's turn, she locates their office building.

The car behind Father honks its horn, and he looks up to see that the Tempo has already pulled away. He drives through the intersection, and on the other side, he slows to let three cars cut back in.

Three junior personnel and two temps greet Father in the hallway with smiles and good-mornings before he reaches his office and shuts the door. Social niceties toward management have become more intense since the downturn, and they make him uncomfortable.

A handful of internal emails wait in his inbox and he needs to second proof a RFP for Monday meeting, but before getting down to work, he searches online for a replacement rowing machine. Used exercise equipment isn't worth fixing, he's learned. He's broken footrests on two rowing machines in the past year, and both times, replacement was simpler than repair. Every second home in Ottawa seems to hold forgotten exercise equipment taking up space in the garage, and buying used just makes sense. Two rowing machines, three treadmills, and a stationary bicycle–Father has bought them all second-hand online.

While scrolling down through Kijiji listings, he picks up a hand-grip he found at Mountain Co-op and squeezes one hundred and eighty repetitions before switching hands. He's been using the things for nearly a month now, strengthening muscle in his forearms to match the size and density of his uppers arms and shoulders.

Through email, he puts in initial bids on three rowing machines, and then he googles *motionless seizure* (684 results found).

Thursday at the RBC, while standing in a long serpentine line that curls three times, Father spots homemade donation tins along the service counter. Beside each teller window sits an empty apple juice can wrapped in purple construction paper, the words *for our Maddie* written in a curling feminine cursive across the side. A laminated index card is placed next to each can, and when his turn at a teller window comes, Father reads that the fundraising is for a local daycare to purchase toys, books, and art supplies–collected *in honour of a deceased girl who gave her parents four precious years that they will forever cherish.*

The index card doesn't say how she died or what prompted the parents to collect money in her name, but Father thinks it must be some sort of coping strategy. Maybe the advice of a therapist or grief counsellor.

As arranged, he picks up his ProGlide Paddler from a suburb in Gatineau straight from work on Friday, and he's set up in the basement by six. After a week without the rowing machine, his shoulders and chest feel different, and though he reasonably knows that seven days isn't enough to really lose muscle density, he decides to forego the treadmill and bike routine in favour of extra rowing.

When he started to take his exercise routines seriously, his key problem was one of proportion. Two straight months on only the treadmill resulted in defined calves and hard clumps of muscle in the upper legs, but there was still a great deal of excess flesh in the inner thigh. The stationary bike addressed those. Then, however, he had to think about his upper body; the extra ten to fifteen pounds were gone, but his chest and stomach were still loose. He was thin, yet not toned. The addition of the rowing machine pretty much took care of everything.

Water bottles within reach of the Paddler, he puts in disc four of season seven of a cable drama. Three fifty minute episodes for a total of two and a half hours. He begins to row.

Sunday morning, he checks his home email and notices two messages from Karen. The first message is to set up a time to meet with the lawyer handling the divorce. Since no assets are in dispute, they are using one lawyer to complete and file all the necessary paperwork. The second message is a request to answer the first.

When he logs off without replying, MSN takes him to a crowded menu page of current events, entertainment news, and relationship advice. An animated sidebar invites him to an online seven card draw tournament, and he imagines Samantha and Laney Wilson living in Windsor. Both of them possess that easy, youthful loveliness that doesn't cross the line into an intimidating beauty and both of them know how to keep up a meaningless patter of conversation, so they make ideal dealers at the middle-dollar tables. With salary and tips from the casino, they don't have to work more than fifteen hours a week, and so they've managed to finish off their undergrad degrees ahead of schedule. Practical for the future, Laney has switched faculties and takes classes in the Paul Martin Law Building. Less practical, Samantha is doing an MA in Social

Work. Their place is the ground floor of a house tucked under the Ambassador Bridge, close to the campus libraries and a straight-forward bus trip to the casino. They share a big kitchen, but with their staff discounts, they wind up taking most of their meals at the casino buffet, which offers a healthy vegetarian alternative every day. In the summer, Laney and Samantha both jog along the river, glancing occasionally across to the American side and feeling relieved that they don't live in Detroit.

In the Google toolbar, Father searches *insomniac narcoleptic* (46 results found).

He and Karen were careful parents right from the start. They attended labour classes and infant first aid workshops. As Samantha grew, they worked hard to make her environment not just protected and secure, but also engaging and stimulating. Words charts and bilingual audiobooks. Swimming and gymnastics classes. An Arts and Crafts camp for the whole family. Weekend daytrips in the city to the Nature Museum and the National Gallery and long weekend trips to the Metro Toronto Zoo or Niagara Falls.

They approached parenting carefully and they always made sure their daughter knew she was loved. The truth was that they didn't need to work quite so hard. When young, Samantha had been an easy, sociable child. They thought they had gotten lucky.

It wasn't until adolescence that she started to withdraw—went straight up to her room after school and wasn't interested in week-end outings. They didn't want to overreact, and they agreed not to; such things were to be expected in adolescence. They did not overreact in the ninth grade when they discovered cigarettes in her purple sequined knapsack. They did not overreact in the tenth grade when she had to repeat a semester of Accounting. Didn't everyone smoke cigarettes at thirteen? And other than accountants, who really needs Accounting? In the eleventh grade, the principal found Samantha's rolling papers during a locker search and gave her a two-week suspension. During those two weeks, Karen found an empty condom wrapper between the chesterfield cushions in the family room. It was time to overreact, they agreed. But they could not agree on how. A serious talk and no more boys in the house–and then what? Grounding? No more television? No more cell phone? No more internet?

Private girls' school? Father thought that was going too far, and when Karen came home with brochures from an *alternative residential school for young women with behavioural challenges,* they began to argue. It was an argument that stretched out over weeks. All kids go through some sort of trouble, he said. No, he was not coddling her, and yes, he had read through the school brochure closely. It was written in aphorisms like *rigid structure* and *formative experiences,* and frankly, it scared him to think of Samantha in such a place. She was just going through a period of adjustment and they should wait. They should just wait it out.

Off-site training has dropped significantly in past couple of years, but this week Father is downtown for development and communication workshops. It's junior management and senior personnel only, so he has known most of the faces seated around him at the conference table for quite some time. They talk work with him, and he talks work with them. They know little of him outside the office, and he knows little of them outside the office.

At some time in the middle of afternoon PowerPoint on Tuesday, his mind drifts away from the facilitator's message, and in the dimmed light of the seminar room, he looks closely at each of his colleagues. Each and every one of them said something last year when he started losing the weight. Good for him. The determination is admirable. It's going to cost a small fortune for new business casual wardrobe. But none of them said anything when he'd stopped wearing his wedding ring. Either they'd not noticed, or they had noticed and they did not feel comfortable mentioning the change. This is what isolation is, Father thinks.

Downstairs from the office tower training centre is a shopping mall where he has been taking his lunch all week. On Thursday, he spots two grey-haired women wearing similar windbreakers, one in yoga pants and the other in sweats. Mall walkers. At one time, he thought such exercisers were fictitious, a satire of the elderly in some mean-spirited version of humour, and so the first time Karen pointed out a group of retirees lapping the food court, he was genuinely surprised. And then, last winter when his first treadmill burned out, Father immediately thought of mallwalking.

This was in January. After an hour of brisk treadmill jog at five point five miles an hour, he had felt confident enough to increase his speed to six point five. It was something of a sprint, but much to his delight, he found that he could do it. He was running. He hadn't run in decades. It was wonderful. His breathing was a heavy pant, but settled into a steady rhythm, and he felt he could keep it up for a good while. Then, something inside the treadmill motor scraped. It was a screeching sound, followed by a turning thump before the tread slowed to a halt. He'd run for all of five minutes. The stationary bike and rowing machine still hadn't occurred to him at this point, and it would take at least a week to locate and get hold of another used treadmill online. So he walked the Bayshore Mall. Two laps of the concourse, up the stairs for two laps at street level, up the stairs again the mezzanine, and down the escalator to repeat.

He worked out a good routine quite quickly, but he missed the television. Without a distraction, he couldn't help but take sideward glances into the Gaps, Roots, and Cotton Ginnys where he inevitably spotted pairs of young women working together. Refolding sweaters or counting receipts, they chatted away with smiles on their faces no matter what they were doing, and it was then that he first imagined his daughter and Laney Wilson somewhere else, working together in much the same happy manner.

Laney Wilson. Karen was the one who mentioned the name first. She and Father were in bed and finished with their books for the night, the lights out for no more than a minute when Karen admitted she'd been monitoring Samantha's cell and email. The news was a bit depressing, but he didn't say this. In truth, he thought invading her privacy was probably a good idea. He didn't say this either.

Even with Samantha withdrawing over the past few years, they knew most of her close friends, but Laney Wilson was new. According to Karen, the girl was now Samantha's most frequent contact name, and they were texting back and forth a dozen times a day. The texts weren't saved, so who knows what they contained, but Karen said the history on Samantha's call log showed messages sent and received as late as two and three in the morning. In the deleted email folder, Karen discovered that Samantha had not been to her driver's education classes the previous weekend, but had instead arranged to meet with Laney Wilson at a used bookstore in the Glebe.

Father and Karen didn't know what to do next. Should they ask their daughter about it outright? Confronting her meant they would have to confess to spying, which would only have made matters worse. Samantha at sixteen was private above all else. He pointed out that all teenagers have poor sleeping habits. And who didn't skip driver's ed classes? Did they have to do anything really? Maybe it was best just to keep monitoring her cell and email. Maybe, he said, it was best just to wait.

§

The commute to off-site training does not include the Greenbank and Fallowfield intersection, and for this, Father has been grateful. The Riverside route he's been taking all week, however, does include a winding stretch along West Hunt Club Road, where the lanes inexplicably bend left, right, left, and then right. Why the road was not constructed as a straight line is a mystery only city planners know. He is more interested in the roadside memorial.

At the sharpest bend, someone has commemorated a deceased loved one with a white cross leaning against a tree trunk off the side of the road. A car crash of some sort. Flowers that are obviously plastic are draped over the cross and a book with a dark cover rests against the base. Probably a bible. He wonders about the nature of the crash, and the number and age of the victim or victims. The mourning loved ones who set up the memorial—do they visit the site often? How do they get here? There is neither a walking path nor a soft shoulder along this stretch of West Hunt Club. Do they come here instead of visiting the gravesite, or do they go see both during the same trip?

Late Friday night after exercise, he googles *non-denominational atheism* (18 results found).

At the Mountain Co-op, he purchases a set of eight-pound ankle weights. Initially, they make the treadmill jog difficult, but by Sunday, he feels that his body will eventually adjust. The effort to lift his legs is greater and he spends more time to travel the same distance, but this is progress. This is what moving forward feels like.

When he wakes for work Monday, he stands and feels a bounce in his legs. It's the weights. His calves, and his thighs, and all those muscle memories have been tricked by the extra sixteen pounds. His first thought is to wear the weights to the office, but he doesn't own socks that will stretch enough, and he decides to simply stay home. Only five of his twenty vacation days can be carried forward to the next fiscal year, and he may as well stay home on the treadmill until dinner.

On Google, Karen located over three hundred Laney Wilsons, seventy-eight lived in Canada, and twenty-eight had Facebook accounts. Since Laney Wilson was a teenager, it wasn't likely that any of the dozen LinkedIn profiles belonged to her. One of the Laney Wilsons on Flickr was definitely from Ottawa, and she seemed to be in the right age range, but all of her pictures were black and white photographs of old people's wrinkled hands, and Karen just couldn't see such a person as Samantha's friend.

When she told him what she'd found, Father wanted to point out the senselessness searching Google and Facebook and Flickr. With such an excess of information, it would be harder to find something that wasn't there than was. *Near-sighted blindness* (813 results found). He didn't say this.

Although Father still maintained that they should wait, she did not, and in the end, their resolve not to confront Samantha with Laney Wilson lasted no more than two weeks. They chose a day when she was home with them for dinner, and as they'd discussed, they approached the topic carefully and made sure she knew she was loved. Even with such precautions, they expected she would feel her privacy had been invaded and they expected an argument.

They didn't expect her to laugh. Shaking her head in amusement, Samantha told them they knew nothing. Anyone can create a gmail account in any name, and anyone can create any contact name on a cell phone. It was absolutely hilarious how little they knew.

With committee interviews scheduled all afternoon, he knows he can't stay home Tuesday. Also, two unscheduled vacation days in a row would disrupt too many of his colleagues. Even before Father goes in, though, he's decided to stay home Wednesday.

During the interviews, his whole body aches and he twice loses his balance as he stands to shake an applicant's hand. Either no one notices, or they notice and choose not to say anything. The position is a one-year maternity leave replacement in payroll. Since the downturn, all new hires are contract positions and holding interviews has become much less enjoyable. Applicants are generally too qualified. Ottawa has always been an over-educated city, but now, more and more of the candidates are older as well. Men and women in their thirties and forties whose curriculum vitae already include first and second careers.

The one recent graduate appears late in the afternoon, the final interview of the day and the niece of someone senior in Human Resources. The interview is simply a workplace courtesy, and in truth, the young woman has little-to-no chance at the position. She is prepared–knows about company policy and structure, and provides concrete responses to behavioural and situational questions–but she is overly timid throughout and avoids eye contact. Father's last question is *what places you above other applicants,* and the situation feels cruel. This young woman will look back on the interview, he thinks, and she will wonder how she could have responded to the committee questions better.

He cannot help think of Samantha, of course. In all of his imaginings, he has pictured his daughter and Laney Wilson thriving. The Samantha of his mind has grown beyond her awkward teen years and is headed for success. She leads an active and healthy life. She's biding her time and waiting to contact her parents once again.

Alone in the office at the end of day, he googles *restless coma* (27 results found). He has yet to find a search with no results.

Karen wanted to punish Samantha for Laney Wilson–take away the phone, the laptop, cancel cable in every room in the townhouse. He reluctantly pointed out that they didn't have a clear reason for these punishments. Besides the crime of invention, what had their daughter really done? They were the ones who had invaded her privacy, they were the ones who had fallen for their daughter's trick. Laney Wilson was like a character in a decoy diary, he said, and they were the ones who had read it. In the end, they gave Samantha one weekend in the house for the missed driver's ed class.

As he'd feared, Samantha continued to withdraw from them. The few times she talked to them at any length, she still seemed to be laughing at them. Arguments and tears made little difference, and over time, the household settled in to a quiet, uneasy truce.

She left without word a few weeks before her eighteenth birthday. The officers that came to the house were sympathetic, but given her age and record at school, they reasonably assumed that Samantha had run off, which he and Karen couldn't dispute. The police would certainly follow up as best they could, and other parents in the same situation sometimes hired private investigators or managed to track their children down online. Most times, though, the best approach was wait and see.

Karen moved out of the townhouse six months later.

Driving home, Father is still thinking about the interviews, and he decides to stop off at a Canadian Tire for five-pound wrist weights. The detour means he's taking a different route home, and as he drives down Merivale, he passes industrial parks that back onto business parks and commercial parks, a hardwood flooring distributor and a Judo studio next to the Silver Dollar Gentlemen's Club. This is not a prosperous part of Ottawa.

On his right, he passes a small church and adjacent cemetery. Both are old, and Father imagines the cemetery has been closed to new business for some time. The rows and columns of headstones are complete, and there's simply no room for anyone else. At the far end, a gravel road running through the rows meets with Merivale, and there at the curb are two garbage cans, a recycling blue box, and one of the city's new green composting bins. How do the dead produce such rubbish, he wonders, and why should there be so much of it?

Wednesday, when the cardiac arrest occurs, Father has been on the treadmill for a little over two hours. With both the ankle and wrist weights on, he can't do more than a jog at four point five miles an hour, but he has worked up a sweat and his pulse is racing. He's planned poorly, and the HBO DVD series he's watching ends. After twenty minutes of supplementary behind-the-scenes features, he switches to broadcast television and a serialized program about a colony of ring-tailed lemurs, monkey-like creatures he remembers from a trip to the Metro Toronto Zoo with Karen years ago. Samantha was in her stroller then, and she laughed and clapped at the lemurs' frenzied leaps and springs within their wire net cage. *Lemurs are nuts.* Part documentary and part drama, the program features a voice-over narration that anthropomorphizes the colony into a family structure, bestowing the animals with more personality they than probably have. Actions that the narrator calls thoughtful parental characteristics are most likely no more than evolutionary behaviours. Until Father's mind wanders, though, the show is a welcome diversion.

What he imagines is Samantha and Laney Wilson settled in Calgary, where they relocated the summer after their undergraduate convocation. The move was Laney's idea. With good sense and even better foresight, she predicted the greater opportunities for employment out west, and she understood that the economic outlook in Ontario would not improve any time soon. Laney Wilson looked out for Samantha and encouraged her to come along. They've put their graduate school aspirations on hold for the time being; their parents' generation celebrated the importance of education, but such wisdom has turned out to be questionable. Many in their forties and fifties now will be underemployed until the day they retire. Not Laney Wilson and Samantha. With Microbiology, Laney works as a regional coordinator for a large pharmaceutical branching out into vaccine study, and with Sociology, Samantha has been hired on by the same company as an internal professional development counsellor in Human Resources. With generous salaries, comprehensive benefits, and an exercise facility in the building, the firm has established itself as one of the fifty-most desirable employers in Alberta. It offers its staff a wide range of activities organized by team, department, and company social committees. For Family Day this year, the firm has acquired the Calgary Zoo, where grandparents, parents, and children are happily tiring themselves out moving from one display to the next. Only a handful of the younger unmarried employees like Laney Wilson and Samantha are in attendance, but they are taking great pleasure in the day all the same. The weather is clear, and they have always enjoyed one another's easy company. At the lemur display, they stand well back from the plexiglas wall, letting a dozen or so of their colleagues' preschoolers and preteens laugh and jostle one another for a better view of the animals leaping and springing frantically inside their enclosure. The animals are cute, Samantha thinks, but the children are truly adorable. In fact, she isn't even looking at the lemurs when her Father's heart arrests; she is looking at all those energetic children and thinking about her future.

GESTATION

I'm about to sign out early and meet Chloe for our second ultrasound, but I refresh my inbox one last time before shutting down. *Subject: New Phone?* The message is from Gillian. Ever since my thirtieth birthday a few years back, she's been writing every month or so. She's called a few times too. That first message was a shock. I don't use any of those social networking sites—I'm an adult and I've got things to do—so I hadn't realized how easy it is for former friends, estranged family members, and ex-girlfriends to track one another down. After seven years of dating and seven years of absence, the unexpected appearance of her name gave me pause. My hands on the keyboard had a slight tremor.

Today's message isn't quite so shocking, and in fact, I've been expecting it.

Isaac—At work and we're pretty busy today and I can't write much more than a few words. Have you changed your phone number? I called on the weekend (no particular reason) and I got a no-longer-in-service message. Did you forget to give Ma Bell her pound of flesh? Did you socially mobilize to second-home ownership? What gives? Hugs—Gill.

With the baby coming, Chloe and I felt we needed more than just the three-bedroom townhouse, and we did, in fact, relocate. The townhouse was originally meant to be a starter home investment property, and if Chloe hadn't grown attached to our suburb, we would probably have moved earlier. As it turned out, the house we wound up buying is on the same street—from one end of Glenmeadow Drive to the other. A five-bedroom with a main-floor office that will give us a quiet place to work once the baby is born.

For whatever reason, I resisted communicating news about the baby or the house to Gillian, and at the moment, it feels like too much to get into. As of late, I've become convinced that Gillian cheated on me while we were together–also too much to get into–and right now, I'm running late to meet Chloe.

"You notice how many new storage businesses there are lately?"

A one-storey cinderblock building, the medical imaging clinic is located in a business park at the fringes of the suburbs. Heading out there, we've driven past three new storage facilities so far.

"U-Store. King's Storage. And now there's a Carleton Warehousing."

Chloe is applying a new coat of lipstick in the visor mirror and not really listening. Ever since the first trimester, she's grown self-conscious about her appearance.

"Businesses seem to be closing down all around Ottawa, so how can self-storage places be flourishing?"

"The Mitchells rent one."

"Really? What for?"

Chloe shrugs.

"Nineteen weeks today," she says.

"I thought only serial killers rented storage lockers."

The ultrasound waiting area is filled mostly with pregnant women and their significant others, but there is one older man here by himself. He's got to be in his seventies, and I can't help but feel for the guy. An ultrasound at his age can't be good news, and on top of that, he's got to sit around waiting with happy, happy soon-to-be parents.

"Nineteen weeks. Do we want to know?"

Chloe is flipping through the pages of a baby furniture catalogue, but not really looking at any of it.

"We should decide."

We've been having this conversation for the past three weeks. If all goes well, today is the day we can learn if we're having a daughter or a son, but we haven't yet decided. Truth to tell, Chloe is the one who hasn't yet decided.

"It doesn't matter, of course," she says.

"Arguments for?"

"It'd make your parents happy. My sister says it'll be easier to plan the shower and come up with a gift registry. And it'll feel more real to you."

This is something the doula that leads our parenting classes said. While mothers experience parenthood from the first pangs of morning sickness, fathers often don't feel attached to the child until they learn the gender.

I shrug. "And against?"

Now it's her turn to shrug. "My parents didn't know for me or my sister," she says, "but I guess that doesn't matter either way."

"So we want to?"

"We do." She nods to convince herself and flips through the furniture catalogue some more. "A couple of girlie pink things or boyish blues wouldn't hurt."

"No, that's fine."

We've agreed that once all the boxes from the townhouse are unpacked, we're going to paint the baby's room a pastel yellow. Neutral and free of gender assumptions.

"Can you put up those shelves this weekend?"

"Yes."

"Sorry I can't help more."

"Not at all."

On our obstetrician's advice, Chloe has avoided lifting anything over ten pounds, which meant that during our move from one end of Glenmeadow to the other, anything over ten pounds was left to me.

"You're done in the basement?"

"Yes."

"Wish I could help more."

"Not at all."

It was while organizing the basement that I became preoccupied with Gillian's fidelity. On top of the boxes of university textbooks, old leases and warrantees, the milk crates of LPs, and all the other crap people can't ever bring themselves to throw out, I have a box of photo albums from my time with Gillian. Instead of just stacking the thing with all the other boxes, I went and opened it. Can of worms. I spent over an hour paging through all that nostalgia.

I remembered a great number of the photos, of course—the shot of Gillian and me in Niagara Falls beside one of those twenty-five cent binoculars, the one of her with her first driver's license, a couple of photo booth strips.

Most of the snapshots showed Gillian alone, but others contained former friends and forgotten acquaintances. Gillian and Stephan Leroux sitting on our patio strumming guitars together. In second year, we rented the first floor of a house where Stephan had the upstairs. He was always rehearsing with that band of his. Another picture showed Gillian in a period costume with Mr. Warchuk after some grade eleven or twelve play, her arm slung around her drama teacher's shoulder. The last picture I looked at was a group picture at Canada's Wonderland, the summer before university. Thirteen wet classmates standing pressed together by the exit to that Timberland Express log ride thing. Danny Maynard, Philip Connors, Sheila Something, Tina, Yuki. I couldn't name any of the others soaked by the water ride. I did notice that Gillian's damp golf shirt stuck to her chest, revealing a dark shadow of brassiere.

She probably cheated on me, I thought. That was enough for me to put the box away, but I haven't been able to shake my suspicion. Once the notion was planted in my head, it couldn't help but grow.

Driving home from the clinic, Chloe holds printouts, and she reviews the features that the ultrasound technician highlighted for us.

"Shoulder and upper arm," she says

"I saw the hand clearly."

"That grey was the stomach."

Most of what we saw in the ultrasound was grey smudges and shadows. In the room, a video monitor was mounted high and angled down, and the technician occasionally froze the image to point out internal organs.

Near the end, the guy asked if we wanted to know the gender. That's how he asked. We. As if he had some stake in the matter.

"The technician guy gave me the creeps," I say.

"Used far too much wavelength gel."

"I noticed that."

"My stomach still feels slimy."

We might not be this critical of the guy if he'd been able to tell us girl or boy. He did try repeatedly, but nothing worked. *The little one is camera shy. The little one is turned away from the monitor. The little one seems to be sitting cross-legged.*

"Next time," I tell Chloe.

Gillian owned a guitar for as long as I knew her. It was left behind in the garage when her father moved out, and she claimed the instrument as her own. The thing was dragged from her childhood home to the apartment of her adolescence, and then her first year dorm, but for whatever reason, she didn't consider using it to play actual music until our off-campus place. Exiting through the shared front hallway one morning, Stephan Leroux happened to see the guitar case leaning against the closet door.

His band was called Goat Dance, but it used to be Horizontal Goat Dance, and before that it was Horizontal Love Goat Dance. The name hardly mattered. Their playing was that kind of repetitive strumming that blurs all genres into one folksy campfire sing-a-long.

In what I remember, Stephan and Gillian met for their guitar tutorials on the screened-in porch, sitting on an old sectional couch left by former tenants. I can still picture the two of them sitting there trying to play in tandem.

In what I imagine, though, the sag in the middle of the couch makes them lean into each other. Maybe they laugh at the discomfort, and Stephan suggests they move the lesson upstairs where she hunkers down on the floor of his room. She's got the guitar propped in her lap, and Stephan squeezes in behind her, his arms reaching around to show her proper finger placement. He walks her through a few bars of music, moving her fingers over the frets, and as she plucks with her other hand, he slips his free arm around the front of her stomach. Without speaking, she leans back into him and feels him hard against her back. Her fingers on the guitar stop, and she turns to put her mouth on his.

On the obstetrician's advice, Chloe has been avoiding strong chemical fumes, which meant the painting of the baby's room fell to me. Not that I minded. The doula says such nesting helps the father feel more attached to the child.

When the paint dried, neither Chloe nor I was thrilled with the neutral yellow.

"It looks like a nondescript waiting room."

"A dental clinic waiting room."

"A strip mall dental clinic."

Our hope was that one of those decorative borders or an accent colour would give the room some character, so today we're putting wallpaper trim. Most of the designs at Colour Your World were Disney or Nickelodeon or Baby Einstein, so we settled on geometric shapes. Neutral and free of corporate interference. The design has these small clusters of cartoon triangles, circles, and squares. Cute enough, but not cutesy.

"Should we draw a pencil line or use the level?" Chloe asks.

"It's probably not necessary."

The wallpaper trim is peel-and-stick, and since we're placing it high against the ceiling, there's no need to measure. If Chloe and I both take an end and stand on chairs, it should go up one, two, three.

"Is your balance all right?" I ask.

"I think so."

Chloe tries not to touch the fresh walls as she stands on the chair and reaches up.

"My centre of gravity is off," she says.

"Want the step ladder?"

"I'm all right. I think."

We manage to put up one strip of trim along the inside wall, and Chloe wants to sit for a break.

"The part near the front will be tricky."

The baby's room has a wide bay window to the street. We figured the light would keep the room warm, but it'll be hard to put the trim up there without wrinkles or creases.

"I just want to sit a minute," she says.

"Did you notice that container thing across the road?" I point out through the bay window.

"Yes. The Donaldsons."

Two doors down and across from us, a massive metal box sits on the driveway. It looks like one of those cargo shipping containers from the docks. The logo on the side says *PODS.*

"Are they moving?" I ask.

"Maybe they just need more space."

"Do you think PODS is an acronym?"

Chloe doesn't respond.

"Their wagon is blocking the sidewalk," I say, "and their other car is on the road."

"I'm sure it's not permanent."

This is a recent compliant of mine, but Chloe has already tired of it. Though the driveways are plenty big enough, everyone at this end of Glenmeadow Drive seems to park on the street. Some of the families have three vehicles, and a few homes have power-boats in the drive–covered in tarp and parked on a trailer for who-knows-how-long.

"I don't understand why people don't use their garage."

Our break stretches out past ten minutes, and in the end, Chloe says maybe she shouldn't stand on the chair again.

"Sorry I can't help more, Isaac."

"Not at all."

"Why don't I call my sister to come over tomorrow?"

"It's all right. I think can do it myself."

Back at my desk after lunch, I find a new message from Gillian waiting for me. *You There?* I stop myself from opening it.

Because she first tracked me down through my work email, her messages always arrive while I'm in my cubicle in the Department of Agriculture, and though I hate to admit it, they usually mean I don't get much work done.

After that original email, I asked Chloe if it was all right if I replied. It seemed safe enough–Gillian lives in Calgary at the other end of the country–and at first, the contact was great. Seven years together and seven years apart, that's a lot of reminiscing and a lot of catching up. I'd forgotten how she made me laugh–how she made me laugh by ridiculing nearly everything. She reminded me what asses we were in grade eleven when we rolled joints with orange pekoe tea and smoked three of them before giving up. She mocked my predictability, saying of course I graduated from university and went to graduate school, of course, I married a classmate, and of course, we moved to Ottawa for government jobs. The tone of her messages is always playful, so she can get away with saying such things.

It turned out she went through several boyfriends after me. Also predictable, but I cannot get away with saying such things, so I didn't. The sheer number of boyfriends was surprising.

I log out without opening *You There?*

Tenth-grade Dramatic Arts was the first class Gillian took seriously in high school, and the effort was because of Mr. Warchuk. It would be simplistic to say that she was trying to please her absent father, but maybe. Warchuk was balding and thick around the middle, and there was something fatherly in the way he made no effort to hide these failings. Gillian was born confident and her discontent tended to come across as witty, so she fit into drama classes well, and by her second semester, she was trying out for most of our school plays.

The picture of them I have comes from a grade eleven or twelve cast party. Warchuk was the kind of teacher who looked the other way when students let a profanity slip, and he might have looked the other way if one of his actors sneaked in a flask of Canadian

Club into the cast party. Something about Gillian's grin in the photograph is definitely off kilter; I wouldn't be surprised if she was halfway drunk at the time.

I don't know how Warchuk would react if she flirted with him, but I imagine he would be susceptible. How couldn't he be? He must have noticed the way that period costume scooped down at the chest, and he must have noticed the way the creases between her breasts moved with her breath. During all those late rehearsals with Gillian, he must have set aside pedagogy for a few moments, long enough to imagine her unclothed. Maybe when she stayed late to run though that particularly difficult third-act break-up scene, he let himself put his arm around her while he played stand-in for the male romantic lead. Maybe staying in character, they would stage kiss, and pulling back, he would congratulate her for inhabiting the role so very, very fully and place his hand on the skin above her breast.

"Do my waist?"

Chloe's lower back aches almost every day now, and she asks for a massage every night before we sleep.

"Not so light. Rub hard."

I've never been any good at this. Gillian always told me I don't rub hard enough, and I always found it hard to get a rhythm going.

"You have to get a rhythm going," Chloe says.

Her patience isn't what it usually is either.

"Maybe you should bring your pillows to work," I say.

"The chairs are supposed to be ergonomic."

"But?"

"I don't know."

"Have you thought about taking early leave?"

"I don't know."

The maternity leave package at Statistics Canada is generous like most government jobs, but Chloe wants to save the time for after the birth.

"We can afford a little extra time off," I say.

"I don't know," she says. "Rub lower. Like kneading bread."

She doesn't want to talk. According to the doula, sleep often becomes problematic late in the second trimester. On top of the back pain, Chloe has to get up for the washroom three or four times a night. Some grumpiness is to be expected.

"More like that," she says. "Circles."

I've slept on the office futon twice this week. She says it's easier to arrange the back and knee pillows if she has the bed to herself. After a while, I can feel her falling asleep and I soften the massage.

With any luck, she will take off work soon. Maybe it'll mean a couple of extra months of mortgage and maybe it'll mean one or two fewer RRSP and RESP contributions, but in the long run, it really won't matter. We won't even notice the difference. This should make me happy, but it doesn't.

What it makes me think of is something unkind I once said to Gillian. Usually, she was the one to start an argument and to keep it going, but once, I was being critical and told her she lacked ambition. This would have been in first year, after she dropped two classes at Christmas. I would have been twenty-one at the time, and it stings to remember. What did I know about ambition or how it works out over a lifetime? Gillian works for a chemical supply company now. Administrative work. It probably doesn't pay what a government job does and there's probably no maternity leave, but in the long run, what is the difference? From the outside, Gillian, Chloe and I have very much the same job. Anyone walking by our desks would just see someone sitting at a computer screen. Ambition seems very much beside the point.

You There? is still unopened when a new message appears in my inbox. *Voice from Afar.* I'm curious, but I've got work to do.

"Abigail."

"Abby." Chloe shrugs.

"Victoria."

"Vickie. Ewww."

We're having a girl.

"Sophia."

"Sophie. Or Soph. Which is much worse."

Thank God I'll avoid all that competitive father-son nonsense.

"Mackenzie?"

"Mac."

Chloe doesn't like any of my suggestions so far, but that's all right.

"Do you like this?" she asks.

She holds up a small table lamp. The base is carved to look like three primary colour crayons.

"It kind of matches the wallpaper trim."

She shrugs and puts it back down.

Three weeks ago, we bought a crib, change table, and dresser set for the baby's room. The furniture is a lacquered white particle board, so we've been keeping our eyes open for odds and ends to give the room a bit more character. Today, we came to Costco for sundries and wound up browsing the baby section.

"I didn't even know Costco had a baby section."

"I need to sit," Chloe says. "Do you mind if I sit?"

"Not at all."

She parks herself in a display rocking chair. It's that gliding kind and has a matching ottoman.

"A battery-powered baby wipes warmer. Cool." Chloe holds it up to show me the smiling infant on the box. "But why battery-powered?"

"In case of a blackout." I shrug.

We've always liked browsing in stores together, and at a certain point, a Sunday afternoon wandering around a box store became just as good as dinner and a movie. Costco has lots of food samples booths.

"Madeline?"

"Maddy."

"Do you want to sit for a while longer?"

"Few more minutes."

Walking has been hard on Chloe lately.

"Portable on demand storage," I say.

"What?"

"The shipping container thing outside the Donaldsons'. I looked it up online out of curiosity. Portable on demand storage."

"PODS."

"It turns out there are plenty of companies that rent out containers. Another one is call PUPS. Portable units, portable storage."

"What about a Winnie the Pooh wall-hanging?"

"It's still Disney merchandise."

"Yeah, but Pooh has always seemed less crass somehow."

Chloe reaches her hand out, and I help pull her to her feet. Sometimes, when we're out performing these little marriage rituals, I wonder what they'd be like with Gillian.

"Do you want me to get a wheelchair?" I ask.

"No."

Chloe and I have taken to using the courtesy wheelchairs when we shop. Over the past two weeks alone, we've signed them out at Bed and Bath, Home Sense, Staples, and the Loblaws Superstore. I'd have thought wheeling my wife around would feel weird, but there's actually something intimate about it.

"Do you miss shopping malls?" I ask.

"I don't know." Chloe shrugs. "I guess."

I'm not sure when it happened, but the suburban stores around Ottawa are all outlets now, and I do miss the mall. If my Dad was on evening shifts, my mother took me to the mall for a food court dinner every Thursday pay day. I bought my first goldfish at the mall Mr. Pet, my first compact disc at the mall Sam's, and my first book at the mall WH Smith. My first kiss was in the mall video arcade.

Gillian hated the mall. The recycled air, the instrumental music, the inexplicable indoor gazebo and water fountain. It was easy to make fun of, but I don't think that's fair. Real things happened at the mall too.

"What about Emily?"

Chloe shrugs. "She'd get Em?"

"I guess."

In the log ride photograph from Wonderland, everyone is crowded in and looking at the camera, but a few of the guys probably sneaked looks at the girls' wet shirts afterwards. Danny Maynard–the one standing shoulder to shoulder to Gillian–is the one I trusted least.

New to our school in grade twelve, Danny was in a couple of plays with Gillian, and he gravitated toward our group of friends. It's not hard to imagine that he would notice how the cold had hardened Gillian's nipples after we walked away from log ride. It would have been easy for them to make an excuse and beg off the next ride–the Octopus or whatever it was–so they could sneak off together. Taking chances in public excited Gillian. Hiding behind some shrub, she would have held his eyes and wriggled her hand down the front of his jeans, telling him in a murmur that he needed to be quiet. The act wouldn't take long, and when it was done, she'd smirk, proud of herself and pecking his cheek before pulling the two of them back to the group.

She would giggle and tell him not to worry. *Isaac never suspects.*

Emily is upside down. The obstetrician tells us not to worry. Breech position is not uncommon, and the problem may sort itself out. As the due date gets closer, though, we should consider an external cephalic version.

After lunch today, I find thirty-two online videos of the procedure. The set-up for all of the clips is pretty much the same: a doctor and a nurse stand beside a heart monitor strapped to the pregnant woman's swollen stomach. The woman lies on her back with her seated partner holding her hand. Some of the clips are short and the doctor's pressing hands turn the baby in under three or four minutes.

In a few of the longer clips, the women cry in pain. The doctors and nurses pause repeatedly and suggest stopping, but the mothers scream *don't stop, I don't want to stop, I don't want you to stop.* Maternal love, go figure. I watch all thirty-two clips. Although the procedure has only a 65% success rate, all of these videos end with the mother crying and the baby turned. I guess no one wanted to post an unsuccessful procedure.

With only an hour to sign-out, I have to admit I'm not getting any more work done. I'm pretty tired, though, and I wouldn't have been too productive even without the videos. On top of worrying about Emily, Chloe has had me sleeping on the office futon all week, and on top of that, the Gillian nightmares have become a regular thing. Some nights, she's with Mr. Warchuk or Stephan Leroux or Danny Maynard or some combination of the three, but other times, she's with someone random. Adams from

Human Resources or the guy who changes the oil for me, or Ian Donaldson, the prick across the road who still has that massive shipping container parked on his driveway.

Because she's on my mind, I'm not surprised to find a new message in my inbox. *You There?* and *Voice from afar* remain unopened, but the title of this one makes me smirk. *Where in the World is Carmen Santiago?*

Isaac—No news on my end. Have you gotten my last few messages? Your phone number still doesn't work, and I'm starting to worry about you. Truth to tell, I'm thinking about you all the time and it's kind of getting to be an obsession. Obsessed with my high school sweetheart—that can't be good. Anyway. I don't know if you're reading this, but I hope so. Hugs—Gill.

The wise thing to do is delete the message, and I do. I delete it, and I delete the two unopened messages, and then, I refigure the security settings on my email, blocking Gillian's address from the account.

"There's more in the hatchback."

"All right."

"Sorry I can't help."

"Not at all."

Chloe's sister surprised her with the baby shower this afternoon. It was a big affair, apparently—forgotten friends she hadn't seen in a while, extended family members who drove in all the way from Toronto and London, nearly half of her department from Statistics Canada.

"This is the last of it," I say.

The kitchen counters are covered with boxes and gift bags. Larger presents crowd the floor.

"Lots of sleepers and swaddling blankets," she says. "But not too many other doubles."

"That is a lot of gifts. You look exhausted."

Chloe shrugs. "I could use a glass of water."

"Sure."

"We got a very hi-tech baby monitor. Video and audio."

"No wet wipes warmer?"

"Afraid not."

"It was fun?"

Chloe shrugs. "Three people showed me their c-section scars. I think they were trying to reassure me, but it was odd."

The external cephalic version didn't work on Emily.

Chloe shrugs. "I am never showing anyone my scar."

The obstetrician doesn't want to wait until the due date anymore, and we're schedule to check into the hospital Wednesday.

"Any words of wisdom?" I ask.

Ever since we found out about the caesarean, people have been offering bits of unsolicited advice.

"Margaret from work told me to be grateful we're having only one. She had fertility-treatment triplets." Chloe smirked. "Apparently the stretch marks are even worse than the caesarean scar."

The oddest advice has come from the doula. When she found out Emily was breech, the woman suggested Chloe sleep with a bag of frozen peas at the top of her stomach. The cold would encourage Emily to switch positions naturally.

"I'm glad the parenting class is done," I say.

Chloe is removing the baby monitor from its plastic and cardboard packaging to show me the three-by-two inch video screen.

"We can watch her sleep for hours on end," I say. "Better than TV."

"Our own home security system after Emily grows out of it."

Pretty soon, we're taking all the gifts out of their packages—unpacking toys and holding up baby clothes to admire them and imagine how cute, adorable, sweet they'll be on Emily.

"Someone's a worrier." I open a medium-sized box filled with baby proofing devices.

"It's a whole kit," Chloe says.

Inside are dozens of electric socket plugs, doorknob covers, cupboard fasteners, and clips for the Venetian blinds cords.

"Who's this from?"

Chloe shrugs, and holds up the set of five toilet seat locks.

"We have only four toilets," I say. "Who needs this stuff?"

Truth is, of course, I need this stuff. My worry has increased ever since the positive pregnancy test.

"Can't hurt." Chloe shrugs.

After our last obstetrician visit, I went online to watch a few c-sections. Scary, but at least all my worry is now properly focused.

"So much stuff." Chloe shakes her head.

Opened and scattered around the kitchen, the shower gifts look even more numerous than before.

"We can put some of it in storage."

"Maybe the shelves by the dryer."

"I want to sort through it first," Chloe says. "Do you mind carrying it all upstairs for now?"

"Not at all."

Three in morning and I'm down in the basement searching for an infant nesting cot. It's a little chair that vibrates and plays *Edelweiss*. Chloe says the slip cover is bunnies and moons, but it might be puppies and moons. Or stars. A hand-me-down from her sister, who said the thing can settle a newborn in no time at all. Chloe is sure it went downstairs with the shower stuff.

Emily is nine days old, five days home from hospital. As the doula warned, sleep has been four hours on and three hours off ever since the birth—the wonderful, freaking amazing, our hearts-could-not-swell-any-more birth. We were warned about that feeling too, but going through it was something different altogether.

So far, the three of us have been sleeping together, Emily nestled in the middle with Chloe and me encircling her. I woke up an hour ago and couldn't get back to sleep, so I came down here to hunt through boxes. I'm back at work in two days and I really have to fix my sleep schedule before then.

No luck in locating the nesting cot yet, but I've let myself reopen one of the Gillian photo albums, and the snapshots feel like two lifetimes ago now. At least two.

It's hard to look at them the same way. Those photo strip booths were crazy overpriced, I now remember, but Gillian always insisted we get two sets of pictures every time. She probably lost her copies years ago. And Niagara Falls. Half the time, those binoculars didn't even work.

She'll eventually contact me again, I know. Any emails to my work account will bounce back to her with some sort of service provider message, but she'll probably think they're a technical glitch. What with *Mylinkedinfaceclassmate* or some such, Gillian will eventually track me down, and when she does, I'll have to be careful what I say.

AND TO SAY HELLO

Once in the playground, while Sam was asleep in his stroller, I watched a little girl as she collected and repeatedly piled a dozen branches and twigs. It was exactly a dozen. I remember because she kept counting the things over and over again.

"One, two, three, four."

Under the steps of the toddler slide. On the bottom stair leading up to the climber. Beneath the monkey bars.

"Five, six, seven."

She picked the sticks up one at time, making pile after pile–patient and slow until she got to eight.

"Ehnintinleven, twelve."

The girl's mother was seated two park benches down, flipping through a glossy magazine, but we made brief eye contact, grinning when her daughter rushed through the end of her count. It was cute. The girl must have been close to three, I guessed.

"What is it with kids and sticks?" I asked across the playground. We were the only mothers in the park, and it would have felt rude not to acknowledge our shared moment. The woman just nodded and grinned again, though. Pretty sure she didn't hear me.

With an inward shrug, I turned to watch Sam sleep, an addictive habit I'd been trying and failing to shake. He would have been thirteen or fourteen months at this point.

In the background, I heard the girl continue.

"First stick, second stick, third stick."

Ordinal numbers. Advanced for three years old.

"Fourth stick, stick five, stick six, ehnintin sticks."

At some point, she started piling the sticks next to her mother on the bench seat. With all twelve arranged to her satisfaction, the girl hopped up, careful not to disturb all that organization, and set about digging and peeling back the bark from each stick. Mostly small wood flecks, but she got off a few good strips now and then. Throughout, she muttered to herself, narrating her own actions.

"Stick skin peels away, away, away."

It was wonderful, and I couldn't help imagining a time when Sam would communicate so very much. He was a calm infant–settled and napped easily and that was lucky for me, I know–but I looked forward to more back and forth.

"Look at how easy the skin comes off, Mommy." The stick in the girl's hand looked to be birch. "Big pieces."

She passed her mother a satisfying chunk of grey-white bark.

"You did a good job. Yes." The woman flipped a magazine page.

"Like a old scab," the girl said.

A simile. Maybe she was four.

The woman folded the corner of a page and passed her daughter a toque. "Ready for home?"

"I'm peeling skin from the stick."

"Here's car hat. It's bark."

"Dogs bark."

"Yes, dogs bark." Distracted, the woman hunted in her purse. Keys probably. "Dogs bark and the skin of a tree is called bark."

"What?"

"The skin on a stick or a tree is called bark, dear. Different from a doggie barking." She was still hunting for her keys–the damn things really do pick the worst time to disappear down a purse.

"Sticks don't bark."

"No. Sticks don't bark. Sticks have bark." The woman stood from the bench and waved for her daughter to follow.

"A dog's not a stick."

"No, it's not. Let's get down from the bench." Her voice was growing impatient.

"Dogs like sticks."

"I asked you to get down from the bench."

This would deteriorate quickly, I thought.

"Dogs bark."

"Now I am asking you again to get down from the bench."

"Are you mad?"

"We can talk about it when you get down from the bench."

"Okay." The girl slid off.

"We have to go to the car."

"Okay."

"Don't you like coming to the park?"

"Yes."

"Do you want to come to the park again?"

"Yes."

"We have to learn to listen better."

"Okay."

After they were gone, the disgusted look on the woman's face stayed with me. She'd kept pointing at the ground to order the girl down, and I made a mental note to tell Fergus about the girl's confusion later. He and I were still doing such things at that point.

We were in bed when I told him, and it led to sharing childhood memories. Fergus once believed *rack and pinion steering* was one word. *Rackopinion.* I once thought *all intents and purposes* was *all intensive purposes.*

"When I was real little, I used to sing *cucumber, chicken of the egg* instead of *which came first, chicken or the egg.*"

"Sesame Street," he said. "I know that song."

"I remember feeling humiliated when I realized my mistake."

"Humiliated?"

"Yet another childhood peril."

"Yes." I could feel him nod next to me. "Stick, dog, bark."

At seven months old, Sam began making a sound that was probably *mommy*, and a few weeks after, there was *dad*. The pronunciation wasn't always coherent and these words often seemed unconnected to either Fergus or me. But nonetheless–first words. In the next month, no new words came. *In Year One* said benchmarks for speech vary from child to child, the pediatrician said Sam was in the eightieth percentile for height and weight, and Fergus said not to worry. I tried not to.

I was a fearful parent, I knew that. My parents had been fearful parents and I had become a fearful parent. The root cause was no mystery–I had a brother who died of a brain tumour when he was five and I was six. One day after school, his eyes went odd, they took him to the doctor, and that was that. As the cancer grew and created pressure against his brain, he was cross-eyed all the time. There's a word for it, but I can't think of it now. Anyway, those months in pediatric oncology left a mark. My parents grew fearful and they passed that onto me. So fine.

Fergus indulged me–reassured me that all parents check their infants' breathing periodically throughout the night, reassured me that all parents dispose of baby food when the vacuum lids fail to pop loudly enough, reassured me that all parents were concerned about the danger of vertical blind cords. So, of course it was normal to worry about speech development, he said.

Mommy and *dad* started to appear more consistently, and then, at eleven months, there was *duck*. A bit of a non-sequitur, but news nonetheless. Sometimes Grover stuffy was *duck,* sometimes the highchair was *duck,* and sometimes his bath duck was *duck.* But accuracy hardly mattered. There was progress.

And then there wasn't. Shortly after his first birthday cake and family party, Sam stopped using *dad* quite as often. Then, *Mommy* became a rarity. More and more, he reverted to his expressive jabbering or he stared and then turned away as if in introspection. *Duck* dropped off altogether.

In Year One said not to worry, but an extra trip to the pediatrician might reduce my anxieties. The pediatrician said there was no need to overreact, but an appointment with a hearing specialist might ease my concerns. Fergus said not to fear, but a few speech development books from the library might relieve my mind.

"The woman stressed that the important thing was not to worry," Fergus said.

We were in bed, going over our appointment with the hearing specialist.

"Of course."

There was nothing wrong with Sam's hearing, and—as far as the specialist could tell—no physical reason for him to have stopped speaking.

"This is good news."

"Good news," said Fergus. "No coordination problems, no dexterity problems, no mobility problems. No cause for worry."

"Yes. And early intervention will help."

Sam was referred to a speech therapist for assessment.

"And he isn't even a year and a half yet," Fergus said.

"Another ten days."

"Really?"

"The fifteenth is eighteen months."

"If a problem exists, early intervention is the best course of action." Fergus was parroting the hearing specialist.

"You're right," I said. "We don't know if there even is a problem at this point."

"Eighteen months?" Fergus shook his head in amazement–like every parent before him.

We were silent for a moment, and I wondered if I'd done the right thing taking an extended leave from work. Was I depriving Sam of needed socialization?

"Daycare?" I asked.

"Daycare might or might not have affected his development."

That was the answer I wanted, but it wasn't reassuring.

"I'm going to the library tomorrow," I said.

At the hospital, moments after Sam was born and placed in my arms, one of the nurses lifted him away to be weighed and measured. He came back to my arms clean and expertly swaddled, a miniature plastic hospital band on his wrist. *Baby boy Simons. Mother: Cheryl Wright-Simons. 7.6. 11-02 13:20.*

It was so he didn't get mixed up with someone else's son, I realized. The bracelet was attached as a precaution–probably part of some standardized hospital procedure. A safeguard. But it did not make me feel safe. That little bracelet could be snipped right off, so what kind of protection was that? Could it stop some barren madwoman intent on snatching a child? Would it stop some anarchist nurse from switching out identification bands? The bracelet made me worry more.

In the library, I learned that nouns should have been the beginning. *Mommy, dad, bottle, diaper, duck, Sam.* Then verbs, often free floating. *Hug, smile, eat, smell, splash, laugh.* The next step was attaching a noun to a verb. *Mommy hugs, duck swim, diaper smell.* Subject and predicate agreement hardly mattered. From there, adjectives could come like adornments. *Happy mommy hugs, yellow duck swim.* And then, things got complicated pretty quickly.

Subject pronouns before object pronouns. First-person first, third-person second. *He is yellow duck.* Sometimes confused. *Him is a yellow duck.* Conjunctions may be limited to *and* and *but,* but *so* could not be excluded. *Duck swim and splashes.* Tense would be limited to present, and present progressive, leading to simple past. Errors in irregular verbs were a positive indicator as they demonstrated an understanding of tense. *Duck swimmed.*

How would Sam get all this? I knew I was being irrational, but delayed speech meant delayed reading, delayed writing, damaged social skills, poor work habits. Unhappiness.

Dogs bark. Sticks have bark.

After thirty minutes on the play room floor, speech therapist Susan came to no concrete conclusions. Sam was delayed. But he maintained good eye contact. Sam was not initiating communication. But he did respond through body language. Sam was not using the vocabulary he should have. But his sounds were clear.

Sam, it turned out, was a good candidate for the First Words program, which in our case would be *Toddler Talk,* a weekly afternoon class for parents and children, and *Two to Talk,* a weekly night class for parents. Thanks to speech therapist Susan, we got into the classes that same week.

"It's set up like playgroup," I told Fergus after our first *Toddler Talk,* "but smaller and focused."

"Focused on dinosaurs?"

"The dinosaurs were just for this week." I said. "Like a theme."

"Sorry."

"Are you listening?"

"Sorry. Tired. I'm listening."

He'd had a late flight in from Calgary that night, and I was in bed reading the *Two to Talk* manual when he came in.

"The focus is on speech development."

"Of course. Sorry. How many kids?"

"Eight. Two twins. All boys between eighteen and thirty-six months."

"Man."

"It was noisy."

I'd read that delayed children were more prone to tantrums, but somewhere in my head, I must have expected a room full of quiet and inward Sams. This was not the case. The twins were the oldest in the group and looked like they might be downright vicious.

"The play stations are set up to trick the kids into talking."

At one table, there had been plastic dinosaurs of different sizes and colours. A big blue brachiosaurus. Little red raptors. Big green pterodactyls. Little orange triceratops.

"You offer choice to force the child to speak."

"I get it."

"Blue or red? Big or small? That sort of thing."

"Did it work?"

"Not on Sam, no. I'm supposed to listen for sounds that are similar."

"Makes sense." Fergus was nodding as he undressed for bed. "What other themes will there be?"

I shrugged.

"Guys and Dolls?" He grinned as he got into bed. "The Mikado."

"Black tie formal."

He slid under the covers on his side. "Prom night under the Sea."

"The Sadie Hawkins hoedown."

"Your worries?" He snuggled in against me.

"All in check."

"Good then."

"Do you mind if I keep the light on to read?" I asked. I could see the disappointment in his face, but I didn't acknowledge it.

"No, that's all right. I'll face the other way."

And with that, he went to sleep.

After my brother's death, my parents were fearful in any number of ways. Any older child could be a bully, any dog larger than a terrier could be a threat, any headache warranted a visit to the doctor. What seemed to bring out their fear the most, though, was a car.

From the back seat of our Oldsmobile, I more than once heard them repeat their disappointment in other drivers. The automobile brought out the very worst in human nature, they claimed. The most ugly and basic selfishness, carelessness, and aggression. Get someone behind a steering wheel and that's all it took to see what is inside all of us. They never said this with anger, but a sad weariness.

So it makes sense that some of my worst fears had to do with cars. Pushing the stroller to the playground, I glared at any car driving even close to our street's 40 km limit. Drivers turning right at an intersection were a particular hazard because they tended to look for oncoming vehicles to their left, not vulnerable pedestrians to the right. On the road, the *baby on board* sign most often discouraged tailgaters, but other times, it encouraged impatient drivers to speed up and swipe past. Fortunately, none of these dangers ever did lead to an accident, but I still imagined the worst outcomes. The speeding car jumps the curb and runs down the sidewalk out of control. The right turning car clips the stroller and sends it crashing. The passing car cuts back too soon and we're forced into the ditch. From there, I would think of the aftermath. Hours in a hospital waiting room. Long distance calls to relatives to pass on the news. The selection of an undersized coffin. Morbid and indulgent imaginings, I know, but the whole point of irrational thought is that it is irrational.

What I could not imagine was a parent continuing on after such a loss. My parents did, but I could not conceive how.

So, no. I wasn't able to keep my worries in check. But I was able to keep them to myself.

Fergus was good husband for many reasons. The security and the money—people say it's not important and blah blah blah, but screw that. After his move from a management to executive pay scale, whether I worked full time, part time, occasional, temporary, or not at all wasn't an issue. I could focus on Sam. And Fergus was normalcy inside and out. Laid back by nature, he knew when to stay awake and listen, when to shut up and spoon, and when to roll away and go to sleep. As a father, he found a workable middle ground. He wasn't one of the wuss house husbands I sometimes saw at playgroup—four days of stubble in a Reading Rainbow t-shirt and sipping on a juice box—but he also wasn't one of those cold descendants of paternal distance just waiting to pass on their Oedipal nonsense. His easy confidence was a good counterweight to my fearful anxiety.

So fine, I should have appreciated my good husband more.

"You're doing well with him."

"Thanks."

Sam and I were at the water table when speech therapist Susan came over to observe.

"Are you counting your wait times?"

I nodded.

This was one of the tips from the *Two to Talk* manual. After a question, the parent was to hold an expectant expression, wait patiently, and speak only after a mental count to ten. I'd practiced my expectant look in the mirror.

"Good, good."

"He still hasn't said much."

"We're obviously having fun." She was talking to Sam and me now. "And fun is where we start."

It was creepy how she slipped into plural. All three of the speech therapists at *Toddler Talk* did the same thing.

"Booooat," she said. "Buh-Buh-Boat."

She lifted a tug boat out of the water table, and Sam turned toward her.

"Buh-Buh-Boooat."

He glanced down at the battleship in his own hands.

"What's that?" Speech therapist Susan asked.

One stick, two sticks, three sticks. Sam looked back up at her. *Four sticks, five sticks, six sticks, seven sticks.* God love her, she held his eye contact. *Ehnintin.* A ten second wait could feel like ages.

"Is that a boat?" she asked.

Sam stared at her again. I didn't want to watch yet another grueling ten count, so I scanned over the other parents to check their progress. One mother had two airplane puppets on her hands, trying to initiate talk with the dump truck puppet on her son's hand. Another mother described Matchbox after Matchbox and Hot Wheel after Hot Wheel as she placed them in a row, trying to get her son to take a turn.

"Yes, it's a buh-buh-boat." Susan finally said.

Sam held out his hand for the tug boat.

"Here you go."

"Thank you," I said with an overly tender tone. My unintentional proxy-Sam voice.

"Have you been reviewing the class materials with your husband?"

"Yes."

"Good. And you're both using the techniques at home?"

"We're trying everything we can," I said. The *we* wasn't entirely truthful.

She turned back to watch Sam. "He is a quiet one, isn't he? Looks so pensive."

This was Fergus's optimistic take. Sam wasn't delayed, he was taking time to consider his words.

"I've been using the sign language along with my prompts," I said. "I narrate what I'm doing constantly. I keep the CBC on in the background." I felt like a child trying to impress a favourite teacher.

"Socialization?"

"We go to the Cityview playgroup. Twice a week now."

"Good."

She glanced at her watch and turned to address the room.

"Hands on top, that means stop."

"What does that mean?"

"A daycare-type rhyme. All the people at *Toddler Talk* use it."

Fergus was helping set the table for a late dinner while I filled him in on our day.

"Watch." I turned to Sam and repeated the rhyme in a singsong voice. "Hands on top, that means stop."

In his highchair, Sam released the infant crayons from his fists and placed his hands on his head.

"Look at that," Fergus said. "This works on a room full of noisy boys?"

"Like mass hypnosis," I said.

It felt somehow wrong to speak about the class in front of Sam this way. Like I might jinx it. Lately, though, I'd found that I was spending all our time in bed telling Fergus these things, and I sensed he resented it.

"Downright *Manchurian Candidate*." Fergus put the crayons back in Sam's hands. "Here you go buddy."

"It signals the end of activities and the beginning of circle time. All the kids and parents march next door where pillows are set up all over mats. Once we're standing in a circle, one of the therapists says *crisscross, apple sauce*."

"Another useful rhyme."

"This week's theme was transportation. Planes, trains, and automobiles. And boats."

"Still no Sadie Hawkins hoedown, then?"

"Not yet."

"Shame."

"Once we're all seated, everyone sings. *We're sitting down for story, for story, for story. We're sitting down for story and to say hello.*"

Sam looked up from his colouring book with a look of recognition.

"*And hello to Sam,*" I sang, "*and hello to Michael, and hello to Jacob. We're sitting down for story and to say hello.* That's Sam's favourite part."

Sam grinned in agreement and dove back into colouring.

"Sounds like you like it too," Fergus said.

"Maybe." I shrugged. "If you want to go, I'll sit out a week."

He shrugged.

"Susan said it's beneficial."

"Yeah but." Fergus shrugged again. "It's more your thing at this point."

The following week theme's was Aquatic Life–plastic fish, colouring sheets of octopi, crustacean costumes. Not quite Prom Night under the Sea, but pretty close, and I made a note to mention it to Fergus later.

Sam and I were again at the water table, which had become his favourite play station. Inside the water were plastic bath toys and I was trying to draw a question out of him.

"Pour?"

The scoop whale was in my hand, and I was holding my expectant look.

"Pour?"

Sam was holding a crab bucket and waiting.

"Pour?"

He looked like he'd wait indefinitely, and after a while, I felt a bit cruel. You were supposed to find a repeated activity that the child wanted and withhold it as a prompt.

"Do you want Mommy to pour?"

Sam nodded. That was a mistake. The *Two to Talk* manual said to avoid yes or no questions.

"Mommy blew it," I said.

I emptied the whale in defeat.

Across from the water table, the mother with twins was having an even worse time of it than me. She was crouched on a throw pillow next to her sons in a carpeted area between the loveseat and a couple of armchairs. The furniture created a separate play station where the speech therapists always set up the container exercises.

"Open? Open?" the woman said.

The twins each had transparent clamshells in their hands and inside the clamshells, there were plastic mermaids. One twin grunted and banged the thing against the carpet but the other one was just staring at it.

"Do you want me to open?" the woman repeated.

The container exercise also worked by withholding help, but with an extra temptation inside the container. It seemed a bit cruel too.

"Open?"

One of the boys stood and yelled an angry noise that sounded like *murhhe*. Mother or mermaid? I don't know. He heaved the clamshell and connected with his mother's forehead, knocking her glasses to the carpet.

Speech therapist Susan rushed over to help, soothing the angry son and checking that the mother wasn't seriously injured, and like all the other mothers, I looked on in helpless concern. Sympathy, empathy, and helpless concern—that was the entire range of emotion in *Toddler Talk*.

The other son, I noticed, was still staring at the clamshell in his lap, as if his brother hadn't just had a complete freakout. Hair had fallen over the quiet boy's face and in trying to focus on the toy, he had gone cross-eyed. *Strabismus.* That's the word.

Fergus was already back at the house when we returned. A meeting had been canceled, he said, and he thought we could all spend the afternoon together.

"Forgot you guys had the class."

"Yeah."

Sam toddled over to his father in a rush.

"There's a message from your Dad on the phone."

"Did he want anything?"

"Just to say hello. Have you told them?"

"No."

Although my parents called once a week, I hadn't said anything about Sam's delay.

"Want to colour buddy?" Fergus lifted Sam to his lap.

The phone message was exactly what Fergus said. *Just called to say hello.* It was the phrase my father always used when he called. The exact same message ever since I moved away for university and never moved back home. A meaningless phrase really, and I long ago understood that he used it to express all the parental worry for which language is inadequate.

The way to survive the loss of a child, I understand now, is another child. I was how my parents went on.

Fergus never wanted more than one. The topic became a source of tension, but as time went on and Sam grew up, it was only one of many sources of tension. Booster seats, junior kindergartens, private schools, French immersion programs, summer camp, girl-friends, curfews. Any one of these topics could lead to days of icy quiet, and they left a mark. Parenting books like *In Year One* never dealt with such problems.

In the end, and to Fergus's credit, he told me we'd simply grown apart. Another meaningless phrase, but kind. We didn't quite make it until Sam's eighteenth birthday, but almost. That's probably to Fergus's credit as well. We separated when Sam was in grade thirteen, and the divorce was final when he was in sophomore at McGill. Computer engineering. Part of me had hoped he would go into Linguistics or Psychology with an eye toward Speech Therapy. His first few years seemed so critical to me somehow and I suppose I expected they would have a lasting impact on Sam as well. But no.

We stayed in the *First Words* program until he was nearly four. After *Toddler Talk,* the next group class was *Preschool Pairs* and then *Chatterboxes,* but there were also night classes in *Phonetic Reading, Enunciation, Speech through Song,* and a couple more I can no longer name. The breakthrough was near the end of *Toddler Talk,* and after that, whatever was delaying his development simply fell away and he progressed quickly. From two-word utterances to three-word sentences, he hardly seemed to pause and he was using coordinate and subordinate conjunctions. One day in *Preschool Pairs,* Sam took no more than a glance at Susan's clipboard and spotted his own name printed there. He pointed and exclaimed *that's Sam.* He saw a word and connected it to language and to himself and made a sentence out of the connections.

"I'm sure you appreciate how significant that is," Susan said at the time.

I did. Such pre-reading skills are a good indicator of later success. Pretty soon he was pointing to words in his picture books and asking what this one was and that one was. Once he had his alphabet down, we played a game in which he'd hunt down key terms. In the car, we would pick random words and he proudly named the first letter. *Tree, tree starts with t. Squirrel, squirrel starts with s. Mailbox, mailbox starts with m like Mommy.* By the time he began junior kindergarten, he was ahead of the children in his class.

But while I remember our time in *First Words* as significant, Sam seems to have no memory of it at all. So fine. Computer engineering.

In the years immediately following the divorce, I saw Fergus only twice. Sam's graduations. Later, though, when my mother passed, he left a sweet message on my machine. Just to say hello, he said, which made me grin. After that, we called each other every couple of months to catch up, and when my father died, Fergus felt comfortable enough to attend the funeral. The last time I saw him was at Sam and Sarah's apartment. They had us over for dinner along with her parents, and—no surprise—it was to announce their engagement. With everyone in a fine mood and after four shared bottles of wine, we got to sharing stories from Sam and Sarah's childhoods, and I was amazed at how much Fergus remembered.

"The time I had heartburn and Sam got sunscreen from the medicine cabinet?"

"What was that thing he said when he upset?"

"*Naked poopoo, it's not your birthday.*"

"That's right. Whenever he was mad at you, he strung together the worst words he knew. *Naked poopoo, it's not your birthday.*"

Fergus asked me if I remembered the stick, the bark, and the dog, and he hadn't even been present that day at the park. My good husband.

That's fine.

On the day that the *Toddler Talk* theme was farming, Sam and I arrived to find the water table filled with cedar shavings. Suitably puzzled, he turned his head from the tub to me and then back to the tub.

"What happened?" I asked

The look on his face was an adult's bemusement, and I had to hold back a laugh.

"Where'd the water go?"

Without so much as a shrug, he accepted this new turn of events and put his hands in the pool of wood, retrieving a plastic cow and a pig as if he expected they'd be there all along. Kids adjust.

The twins, I noticed, were now accompanied by both mother and father, the whole family sitting at the Play-Doh station, where a dozen farmyard animal molds were scattered. The father didn't seem to be paying much attention, but his presence did have an effect. Working together, the twins produced blue sheep after blue sheep, one brother rolling flat pancakes and one brother stamping the mould into the dough. It was cooperation, all right, but they were still silent. I thought to mention the man's presence to Fergus later, but never did.

"What do you have there?" I asked Sam.

He'd pulled out the bottom of his t-shirt, cradling a half-dozen barnyard animals in the stretched cloth.

"Moo cow," I said. "Oink pig, baa sheep, cluck cluck chicken."

Sam handed them to me one by one–expecting I don't know what. The look on his face was all business, though, so I played along, lining the toys up on the floor in an orderly fashion.

"Neigh horse, gobble gobble turkey."

He bent back over the water table, his arms elbow-deep in wood chips and searched for more.

"Maybe we found them all? No more?" I asked.

I reached to join in the search for a rooster or goat or whatever and came up with a small plastic duck.

Sam grinned. "Duck swimmed."

ON THE APRIL MORNING OF
HIS SECOND EX-WIFE'S PASSING

On the April morning of his second ex-wife's passing, two provinces away, Ronald Kelly walks along Slatterley Road and thinks of health and of aging and of death, reflecting on the linear direction of mortality. Since Kelly will not learn of the death for several hours more—not until he returns home to his two-bedroom town home and listens to all three of his telephone messages—these reflections might be taken as more significant than happenstance, but such a conclusion would be a mistake. In truth, Kelly has the very same contemplative thoughts every time he trudges his aging body along Slatterley Road. On the unhappy days that he journeys to the university to teach a class and on the even unhappier days that he must attend a faculty meeting, Kelly must pass by the Briarfinch Retirement Village, the Glensparrow Assisted Living Home, the Valleymartin Long-term Care Facility, the Central Winnipeg Funeral Parlour, and the Lovingly Used Consignment Shop. These businesses appear in succession along Slatterley, a downhill reminder of the route all life eventually follows, and walking past, Kelly cannot help but consider death's stalking.

This morning, the questions he puts to himself and the thoughts that linger most are connected to the consignment shop. How profitable can the clothing of the dead be? Who might happily purchase the six plate settings of Royal Doulton displayed so prominently in the storefront and not wonder about the elderly woman who collected the individual china pieces for decades? And which, if any, of his own unexceptional belongings and sundry possessions might secure a place of distinction in the shop's front window display after his death?

Such considerations follow him along the two blocks to the bus shelter, throughout his journey, and into the end-of-semester faculty meeting. With his mind thus occupied, Kelly does not listen to much of what his department chair has to say this morning. Something about a redesign of the History Department website and something else about funding for new sessional hires in the autumn, but these hardly matter. Kelly long ago learned that granting such a meeting his full attention just led to unpleasant ruminations and questions. How often does the department need to fiddle with its website? How many middle-aged PhDs can the department exploit with dead-end sessional positions? If it weren't for the extended discussion of each agenda item—propositions and movements that are seconded, thirded, and duly recorded by the department's attractive new administrative assistant—he wouldn't believe any of the professors, lecturers, or grad students in attendance were actually listening either. Kelly cannot quite understand why people want to prolong their time locked inside the seminar room any longer than necessary—asserting self-importance and jockeying for meaningless position—but he shrugs the mystery away. Human nature was not made to be understood.

As he imagines is true for a great many men, Kelly has always found that boredom and restlessness lead to thoughts of a sexual nature—funny that such an impulse hasn't diminished into his sixth decade—and as the faculty meeting heads into its second hour, he watches the new administrative assistant's movements closely. She is seated directly to the chair's left, allowing Kelly to stare and feign attention to the meeting all at once. New to the job, she scrambles to record every suggestion and objection released into the air of the seminar room, her brow crumpled tight and her mouth twisted in nervous frustration. She's on the plump side, but in a flattering way, with a soft face and a considerable chest that she hides under a loose-fitting blouse. At this very moment, Kelly is looking in between the uppermost button of her blouse, where he can just barely make out the shadowed crease of skin where her breasts press together. Who does she remind him of? Not his first wife nor his second but someone from the interregnum. *A special lady friend.* Kelly remembers the euphemism he used to amuse himself with, but he cannot connect the memory of arousal to the memory of a name.

"All right," the chair says, "with item four closed, I will turn the meeting over to committee reports."

Committee reports are most often the reading of the minutes from various other smaller meetings, the goings-on of the speakers committee, the publications committee, cross-discipline appointment committee, and the graduate student society, and it amuses Kelly to think how these minutes will later be minutes with the minutes of this faculty meeting. Minutes within minutes. Fortunately, the reports also mean that unless one of the committee heads decides to drone on at length, the meeting is more than half over. With a rejuvenated magnanimousness, Kelly focuses and listens intently to the names of the guest lecturers who may or may not visit the school in the autumn, to the date and location of the launch party for volume seven, issue three of *Prairie Odysseus,* and to the requirements for a proposed minor in Classical Studies and Ancient Greek History. Last to speak is the graduate student society president, a gangly young man who not only has the misfortune of being the graduate student society president, but has voluntarily held this position for the past three years running.

The presence of graduate students at these meetings has always astounded Kelly. Their attendance is in no way mandatory—or beneficial as far as he can see—and yet, year after year, there is a small contingent of these tired, unhealthy-looking young men and women sitting around the edges of the seminar room. Naturally, once or twice over the years, the sight of these young budding and blooming academics has made Kelly wistful and forced him to think of the opportunities at fatherhood he quickly dismissed and/or wasted in his lifetime, but more often, he focuses upon their foolishness. In all likelihood, the grad student society president views these meetings as a form of social networking, a way of cementing a department bursary or guaranteeing some future letter of recommendation, but such interest and enthusiasm for such nonsense makes Kelly want to grab the boy by the shoulders for a thorough shaking. He wants to tell him to run off to the bar with friends. Argue over a pitcher of draft beer. Take a road trip to the west coast. Find a summer job teaching learning-disabled children kids to kayak.

He says none of this to the graduate student society president, of course, and instead stares at the peeling decal ironed onto the mannish boy's t-shirt. *The unexamined life is not worth living.* It is a quotation that maddens Kelly–not because it is a slogan for a t-shirt, but because of the two negatives, which always seem to be read as an endorsement of analytical self-reflection or critical examination or some such nonsense. The wording is sloppy, however. Asserting that the unexamined life is not worth living does not necessarily mean that the examined life is worth living. *I'm not unhappy* does not mean *I'm happy.* The examined life may be equally not worth living. But then, perhaps the translation is poor.

The t-shirt triggers something. Without his cooperation and independent of his will, Kelly finds that his thoughts drag him along an unexpected path and connect to arbitrary associations. These startling runaway trains of thought are happening more and more, and in a way, they make sense to Kelly. The volume of memories increases as a mind ages, but the facility to manage these memories decreases as a mind ages. A certain amount of unpredictability is to be expected.

Where the young man's t-shirt and decal lead Kelly's mind is the reading room in the Slatterley library branch, where a yellowing poster with peeling scotch tape is mounted to the wall. *Reading Increases Empathy.* Below the wisdom, some contemporary writer Kelly doesn't know and has never bothered to identify is seated in a reading chair holding a burgundy hardcover with no title. Whenever the poster catches his eye, Kelly inwardly nods and agrees that reading may well increase empathy. The educated reading class does tend to be more empathetic. However, a causal relationship isn't certain. Those who naturally possess more empathy may be more drawn to reading than those without.

"Before we close," the chair says, "I want to wish everyone a good summer, whether or not you're teaching or off somewhere on a break. I will be available at the department until the end of May and by email thereafter."

The administrative assistant sighs, looking as relieved as Kelly inwardly feels, and as everyone stands from the conference table, he searches for a passing remark to endear himself–a quip to make her smile and perhaps initiate a conversation–but he can think of nothing. A file folder tucked under her arm, she brushes past, and Kelly is granted one final glance at the uppermost button.

Frances Renault, that's the name he could not locate earlier. Frances Renault, a pleasingly round post doc medievalist who was with the department during Kelly's early years. His first marriage was already winding up at that point, so Kelly's time with her could hardly have been called infidelity. Besides, neither Kelly nor his first wife was able to keep within the confines of marriage, and so neither of them was really at fault. Special lady friends continued into his second marriage as well, but they were not the cause of its dissolution. That nearly amicable divorce was about the children he was unwilling to provide. Fortunately, the second ex-wife was able to secure a second husband and produce two healthy daughters in a quick span of five years, all before the looming deadline of a fortieth birthday. *Well, good for her,* that has always been Kelly's attitude.

These are the thoughts that cross his mind while the faculty meeting in the seminar room winds down, colleagues breaking off into small clusters to share their summer research projects and talk of all the pleasure reading they intend to catch up on as Kelly heads to the elevators to steer clear of such sociable chit chat. He lets himself drowse on the bus, and later, his route again takes him along Slatterley past the string of morbid businesses in reverse. Seen in this direction—uphill from funeral home to long-term care to assisted living and a community of the retired—the walk seems not quite so disheartening, and Kelly feels his spirits lifted.

Indeed, if he were the kind of man to whistle, he would be whistling as he opens the door of his town home and sweeps into the front foyer, jauntily kicking his overshoes onto their mat and hanging his overcoat onto its hook. In the front hall, his obsolete cassette answering machine flashes again and again, a welcoming and digital red *3, 3, 3, 3, 3, 3.* The first message is one of those robocalls, a prerecorded voice selling home delivery subscriptions to the *Winnipeg Free Press.* The now twice-recorded voice is an odd and recent phenomenon, Kelly thinks. Someone else's machine talking to his machine, and his mind connects the message to the meeting-minutes-within-meeting minutes. Recordings of recordings, and in this way, he thinks, history is documented. The second message is also a sales call, and an attractively confident woman's voice offers him cut rates on no-fault car insurance.

And then the third message. His second ex-wife's second husband—now her widower. The identity of the voice doesn't register at first, of course, and the sad news throws Kelly off balance, once again triggering uncontrolled associations that he must struggle to reign in. His mind goes to the proposed minor in Classical Studies and Ancient Greek History—such strange works these synapses do—but then the connection comes to him. Off stage death, that's the damn connection. With the exception of Sophocles' *Ajax,* deaths occur off stage in all the extant works of all three tragedians. *Ajax* is also one of the only instances of suicide in Ancient Greek drama, but Ajax would not have been the title character in the original production. Like all of the tragedies, the title was added by later editors, and the first audience would have known the work by its opening line. *Odysseus, I have always seen and marked you/Stalking to pounce upon your enemies.*

The confusion lasts no more than a second, and then Kelly focuses and replays the recorded message from two provinces away. The second husband has an apologetic voice and explains that he's been calling friends, family, and loved ones with the when-and-where of the service. Of course, he understands not everyone will be able to attend. Donations to breast cancer research in lieu of flowers. Near the end of the short message, the second husband's voice trails off a bit, and Kelly feels a sudden, unexpected empathy and compassion for the poor man. God willing, one or both of the two now grown daughters are staying at the house with him. They can stand by as he makes these difficult telephone calls, preparing tea and holding his elbow gently whenever his voice wavers. Kelly, of course, feels envy along with his compassion.

It is envy because the second husband's mourning this April morning will be lessened by the love of two daughters. Children who will inherit and cherish unexceptional belonging and sundry possessions. And once again, a runaway train of thought takes Kelly by surprise and into a scene from his past.

Near the end of the marriage, in bed after lights out, Kelly and the second wife were holding one another and talking in the soft voices that they both knew would lead to intimacy, for these were the soft voices that had led them to the same place twice weekly since they'd taken their wedded vows. That night, though, their pillow talk was derailed—one of those sudden and inexplicable marital flare-ups—and she somehow wound up asking yet again about children. That was not who he was, he explained. That was not who he was, and that was not how he was made. He reminded her that their positions in this debate were longstanding, and it wasn't long before she was out of bed and crying alone in the ensuite, the bathroom lights leaking out into the bedroom. Kelly remained in bed weighing the value of getting up and going to her, but did nothing. She returned and stood in the open door to ask him why, why, why, and he could not help but notice the way her night dress revealed the shadowed valley between her breasts. He would someday soon miss that sight, he thought, and though Kelly knew he should feel compassion, what he felt was not unhappy.

PARENTS OF CHILDREN

Mornings, between nine and eleven, Gault preferred to pass his time in the dining hall with a book. With the majority of the Woodlawn residents congregated in the common room or out walking the grounds, the dining hall was pretty much the only spot for peace and quiet outside of his suite. If he stayed alone too long in the suite, he tended to chain smoke and nap frequently. The easiest of bad habits. The library was sometimes safe, but the risk there was a lonely soul who wanted to strike up a conversation about a book club selection.

With the kitchen staff taking down the breakfast buffet, Gault settled into the armchair by the window, warmed by the August sun right off. Today the book was a suspense novel he'd been looking forward to–British, with the promise of some crooked perversity. If it was any good, Gault needed no more than ten or fifteen pages, and from there on, he was pulled right in. Time passed all around him and he noticed none of it.

This morning, though, the new woman from the third floor had invited guests for breakfast–a daughter and infant grandchild would be Gault's guess–and the three of them were lingering in the dining hall. The mother and daughter were in some sort of polite dispute and try as he might, Gault was unable to ignore their exchange.

"Just to make the apartment feel a little more like home, dear."

"I understand."

"All the paintings are in storage. Just a few portraits."

From what Gault could gather, the old woman wanted a drive to Home Depot to buy picture hooks, but the daughter was reluctant. A bulky stroller was parked between them, pulled up to the table so they could watch the napping infant. The old woman changed the topic and commented that the baby looked so calm sleeping. The daughter said she wished Brie would sleep through the night like all the other babies in their playgroup. The forced courtesy in their voices was obvious, and Gault bet the topic of the errand wasn't far off. He was right.

"Can we wait until the weekend?" the daughter asked.

"Ten minutes," the old woman said. "Right in and right out."

"Home Depot is never ten minutes."

Gault couldn't help but listen. The daughter said she had things planned and she'd return on the weekend. The mother said it was only Tuesday and the weekend had just ended. The daughter said she could leave Brie with Paul on Saturday and it'd be much easier to run errands.

"Can't Brie sleep in the car?" the mother asked.

The daughter said please, the mother said please, and the daughter stopped being polite.

"I cannot be available to you all day every day."

"Of course, dear."

"I took the extended leave because I regard maternity seriously. I would hope you could respect my decision."

"Of course. You are right dear."

"No one else gets me upset like you do."

"You are right, Virginia, and I'm sorry I upset you."

Astonishing, Gault thought. Astonishing how quickly such matters could escalate between family members.

The two women sipped their tea in silence for a while, and then, the mother asked if the meal was all right. Woodlawn put out only a continental breakfast during the week, but the pastries and the fruit were always fresh.

"I can't believe they have mango and kiwi."

They stayed another half hour or so, and by nine thirty, Gault had the dining room to himself. By ten, he was fifteen pages into the novel and wholly enrapt. A little later than planned, but not too far off schedule.

Located in the southern suburb of the city and advertised as *independent living,* Woodlawn presented itself as a distinct alternative to retirement living and assisted living. At Woodlawn, residents were promised privacy without the responsibilities of running a household–autonomy but no worries about laundry, snow, and front gardens. The dining room served three daily meals and an afternoon snack daily, but each suite came furnished with a kitchenette for residents who wished to dine alone.

Gault moved here when the facility first opened. At the time, he was sixty-six, one year out of the police force. He liked the facilities well enough, but the place did get to him from time to time. In his most desperate moments, he looked around at his pitiable ageing peers and thought Woodlawn's *independent living* meant nothing more than the first slip on a slippery slope. This was where atrophy began, he thought, the first step downward to a wheelchair, days in bed, a franchise funeral home, and a non-denominational memorial service. And in the end, all your crap belongings are sold off to the consignment store down the road.

On the plus side, Woodlawn was one of the few homes that still allowed smoking in its suites, and the place did deliver on its promise of privacy and independence. Ms. Sanderson, the general manager, was a constant presence, but she tended to drift about in the background and didn't push the social activities too hard. She could take a hint if Gault had a book with him. The activities consisted of outings to the zoo and botanical gardens as well as bingo and card nights in house, but none of it was mandatory. Another plus–an actual cook oversaw the Woodlawn kitchen, so there were no boil-in-the-bag meals supplied by the catering multinationals that most retirement homes used.

The woman's name was Aubrey, and Gault learned that she'd moved to her third floor suite some two weeks earlier. She could have been a divorcee, but he guessed widow. Judging from the needy way she jumped to mollify her daughter, he thought she'd probably lost her husband some time ago. At Woodlawn, new residents sometimes took a while to settle into the right group of friends, so it was no surprise to see her still sitting by herself after breakfast clean-up on Friday.

During the few mornings since that scene with her daughter, Gault had acknowledged Aubrey only with a nod, but now was as good a time as any for an introduction.

"Thomas Gault."

"Aubrey Moore."

She extended her hand to shake his, and he smirked, feigning amusement at her the formality.

"May I join you a while?"

"No book today?" she asked.

She had been watching him—he'd guessed as much.

"Finished it up late last night, as a matter of fact."

"And?"

"Very satisfying. Stayed up past twelve o'clock just to get to the end."

"Shocking at your age."

She had a teasing manner that surprised Gault, but pleased him too. She wouldn't bore, at least.

"I mostly stick to mysteries and thrillers," he said. "Sometimes horror stories. People talk about all the great literature they'll read after they retire, but I say nuts to that. Too much like homework."

"I'm sure you're right."

"Aubrey is a splendidly old-fashioned name," he said. "Stately."

"I've always liked it."

"You hear such absurd names around here on visiting days. Grandsons named Brayden and Jayden. Little girls saddled with Madison, Ashley."

"Brianna," Aubrey said. "Alexis."

"Paige. Brie."

"Brie. My own granddaughter is saddled with that one."

"Yes." Gault nodded. "I overheard that."

He checked her expression, but she didn't seem to mind.

"I was not trying to eavesdrop, I assure you," he said. "But as a matter of fact, I overheard much of your conversation."

From his shirt pocket, he removed a half dozen picture hooks.

"Not too presumptuous, I hope," he said.

She shook her head, and with a genuine smile, said the gesture was thoughtful. This was as Gault had hoped.

"You should use small finishing nails when you put them up," he said. "Woodlawn's powers-that-be will go after your security deposit if you put too many holes in the walls."

"Any other helpful tips for a new arrival?"

"Oh, yes. Don't buy into the weekly laundry. Overpriced and they do a poor job of it. The lending library fees are too high and the selection is poor. The video library, though, is well worth the money."

"Good to know."

"And avoid the mall walking club. Complete idiots."

"I should be writing this down." Aubrey smiled.

They lingered in the dining hall most of the morning, refilling their mugs from the coffee and tea urns left out from breakfast. As with many early conversations in Woodlawn, they talked largely about their occupations before retirement. She'd been a social worker for the city and worked out of an office not too far from Gault's precinct. Surprising their paths had never crossed, they agreed. And as it will, talk eventually came around to family.

"Two daughters and a son. Virginia is the youngest," Aubrey said. "Three granddaughters. Brie is the latest. Two step-grandsons, but they're older."

"Two sons here," Gault said. "Five grandchildren. Five and counting from the older son, and none yet from the younger."

"That's got to be quite the expense at Christmas."

The two daughters were tenure track professors, Aubrey said. One in Psychology and one in Sociology, and she liked to think she had something to do with those choices. The son was a radiologist, married to a woman ten years older than he, but that wasn't such a scandal, Aubrey supposed. Brie was an only child, and the two older granddaughters were in figure skating and gymnastics. Both showed great potential on the parallel bars.

"Sorry," Aubrey said. "I'm going on."

Gault smiled and shook his head. "You have good reason to be proud."

"And your boys?"

"Sam and Thomas Junior. One owns a restaurant with his wife, the other is a professional student. Post-graduate studies now." Gault shrugged and nodded as if thoughtful. "They've done well, but I can't take any credit." He shrugged.

In his lifetime, Gault had had a total of five fiancées, but never a wife. His engagements all happened in his twenties and thirties, at a time when he still genuinely believed himself capable of long-term fidelity. To his credit, he did make a go of it while immersed in his successive two-and-three-year relationships; he was faithful right up until the point that he wasn't. As a result, Gault had been on a lot of dates, and while not exactly charming, he'd learned to be a good date. Though he'd never been particularly athletic, physical training for the police force in his day was still quite rigorous, and over time, a fit, muscled body became a kind of habit. A habit that made meeting women all the easier. In his late twenties and thirties, he preferred someone five to eight years younger than he, and such goals were reasonable most of the time.

Some time during his late forties or early fifties, he realized he would have to change tactics; his weight was under control, and he remained strong, but there was an all around thickening to his physique. The change was especially unflattering around his jaw line, where a layer of thick skin hid much of his neck. Charm took a man only so far.

If the many date movies he'd sat through were anything to go by, what women of a certain age found desirable was a sad widower. In fact, Gault noticed that for a certain type of woman, nothing was more desirable in a late middle-aged man than a dearly departed wife, and so, he invented one. The plan worked well. Astonishingly well, really, and it was easy. Beyond the central lie, all that was needed was a sad mention here and there. It was amazing just how little effort was required. A quiet, evasive widower was more appealing than one that chatted on and on about his dearly departed wife.

That Saturday, Gault made toast with jam in his suite and lingered long enough to miss breakfast service. As he'd hoped, Aubrey was already occupied with her daughter Virginia and granddaughter Brie when he entered and poured himself a mug from the coffee urn. Aubrey looked up as he passed their table on his way to the armchair by the window, and they acknowledged one another with a grin.

He settled in with a new novel, but glanced up over top of it just often enough to let her know he was watching. Today, the baby was awake in her stroller, and Aubrey was busy entertaining her with some sort of orange octopus rattle.

From what Gault could make sense of, the daughter was complaining about the women in her playgroup.

"It would be better if I knew someone from the university with a baby. Most of the other parents are ten years younger than I. It's the same scenario in Mommy Massage and Tot Swim. The only woman my age is on her fourth child and has never worked outside of the house, so we really have very little to talk about."

With his mug emptied, Gault closed the book and stood to leave. The daughter's chatter meant there wouldn't be an opening to say hello, which was just as well. As he passed the parked stroller, though, Brie provided him with a stroke of even better fortune. With a giggle, the infant flung the orange octopus onto the carpeted floor. Retrieving the toy, Gault grinned and passed it to Aubrey.

"Here you go, Grandma."

At the dining hall exit, he didn't look back, but knew she was watching him still.

"You were eavesdropping again," she said.

Gault looked up as if taken off guard.

"May I sit?" Aubrey asked.

"Oh, yes." Gault set his book face down on the table.

"Would you rather read?"

"No, no. Not at all."

Gault had arrived early for breakfast today and set himself up at a table in the far corner. She should approach him, that was the reasoning.

"Brie is adorable," he said. "She'll overcome the name."

"Thank you sir."

"But, I'll have you know that I was, in fact, not eavesdropping."

"Noble."

Aubrey smiled, and he invited her to sit. A plate of coffee cakes sat untouched on the table before him, and they nibbled while she told him about yesterday's visit. The daughter Virginia's extended maternity leave was soon running out apparently, and she didn't yet qualify for a sabbatical. Another year off work was possible only if she put in for unpaid leave. It was proving hard to give up full time motherhood, but more time off meant risking her chances of tenure.

"And what did you say?" Gault asked.

"Me? I said nothing. Better to keep some thoughts to myself."

"Yes." Gault grinned. "Not easy to be a parent of children."

"No."

"Truth to tell, your daughter the other day brought my daughter-in-law to mind."

"How's that?"

Gault shook his head. "Last week. And again, I apologize if I was at all eavesdropping."

"Yes?"

"Your daughter seemed on the pushy side."

"Pushy?" Aubrey raised her eyebrows. "A bit pushy. A bit bossy. A bit condescending."

"Don't be too hard," he said.

"Yes, of course." She smiled. "But I don't necessarily need to be scolded just because I try to give my granddaughters a digestive biscuit that may or may not have traces of peanut dust."

"Yes, I've received that particular reprimand myself on occasion."

"And you would think one butterscotch from time to time was going to rot their teeth."

"The last time my older son visited," Gault said, "my daughter-in-law saw fit to lecture me about the dangers of third-hand smoke."

"Third-hand?"

"Apparently the odour of cigarette that clings to my clothing and furniture can be toxic."

"I see."

"What I like to do," Gault said, "is allude to the topic of money. Let them think that you're being careless with their future inheritance."

"That's terrible."

"Oh, it's terrible. But nothing gets the kids' attention more. Makes them lean forward perceptibly. I've seen them do it. And all it takes is a few hints. I tell them I'm moving around a few investments or I'm meeting with a new financial advisor. A representative from Sun Life or the Investor's Group or some such questionable enterprise. Sit back and watch the kids grow concerned then."

"That might work with Virginia. She's terrified of being cheated."

"For you," Gault said, "I would recommend a different tactic. Tell your daughter about a psychic or an interesting medium you saw on the television."

They grinned and fell quiet for a moment.

"Would you like to walk?" she asked. "Outside?"

"What's that?"

"You don't have to spend every morning in the dining hall, you know."

"The grounds are said to be beautiful." Gault shrugged. "And I wouldn't mind a cigarette."

For some women, what was even more poignant than a sad widower was a sad widower left stranded with children to raise. Presented with such a man, some women swooned, and Gault could practically see the admiration growing in their eyes as they imagined him acting as both mother and father. What could be more steadfast and decent than a father alone with dependents? And as with the fictional dearly departed, the invention of children didn't require much. A tender anecdote here or there–about carpooling his younger son Sam's soccer team or disapproving of his older son Thomas Junior's first girlfriend. Gault liked to prepare a few well chosen details and let a woman's imagination do the rest. It was astonishing how much women would assume, really.

The boys had to remain conveniently absent of course–off at school or relocated to another city for work–so Gault didn't start inventing sons until his late fifties. Around this same time, he learned to be more flexible about his five to eight years younger rule as well; the difference between a middle-aged and a late middle-aged woman's physique was negligible anyway, and after a certain point, such matters were better handled with the lights out.

The greatest age difference he ever allowed himself was some sixteen years: when he was sixty-four, he spent nearly a year with a forty-eight-year-old waitress. She could have easily passed for late thirties. Unlike previous relationships, that one ended not when Gault's interest looked elsewhere, but when his ability to perform became unreliable. And he wasn't about to start taking a bloody pill. Not worth the indignity. Instead, he broke off the relationship and shifted his life's focus–took up reading more, relocated to Woodlawn House. Up until Aubrey Moore, he'd managed to keep himself to himself for nearly five years.

While not expansive, the grounds of the independent living home were well cared for, tended to year-round by the home's two Korean maintenance men with occasional assistance from outside landscaping contractors.

"With a name like Woodlawn," Gault said. "They have to keep the place pretty."

That first day, he and Aubrey confined their stroll to the home's property, following the soft gravel path that circled and wound its way around the building. Over the next two weeks, though, when the walk had become part of a morning ritual, they followed the city trails that led away from Woodlawn. The late August weather had turned moderate and lent itself well to slow meandering. Venturing farther and farther each day, they eventually reached the stretch of path that ran alongside the river, and they sat on a park bench to rest.

"Ducks." He pointed down to the river's edge, where five of the birds drifted toward the shore. "Why five? You would think they would travel in couples."

"Perhaps," she said. "We should bring bread tomorrow. I've always loved watching them waddle their little bodies chasing after breadcrumbs."

"Yet another activity my daughter-in-law objects to," Gault said. "Makes the animals dependent upon people for food, and more than that, it doesn't teach my grandchildren the proper respect for wildlife."

"That shouldn't stop us from having our fun," Aubrey said.

Over the past two weeks, the offences of adult children had become a reliable topic of conversation.

They talked about the usual as well, of course. She told him about her childhood, her family, and the decades she spent in social work—the few lives she managed to improve and the many lives she was unable to affect in any way at all. It changed a person over time, she admitted. Conversation sometimes drifted to her husband—who had passed eight years earlier, much as Gault guessed—but she was tactful and shared only a few details about her marriage.

Gault said only that his wife passed early on in the marriage. He talked about his job mostly—juicy cop stories, that's what Aubrey called them, though they hardly were. The time he pulled over a city councillor and didn't let the guy off for speeding, the time he didn't arrest a woman for burying the family dog in a city park. If the subject of family came up too often, Gault fell back on pensiveness and said only that his sons didn't visit much.

"No sense in dwelling." He let his voice drift away.

For Gault, one of the surest signs that he and Aubrey were growing closer was how much time they spent making fun of other Woodlawn residents. Absent-minded Douglas Crane, who seemed to have toilet paper stuck to his shoe for days on end. Hair-net Margaret Meadows, who wore nothing but tropical flora-and-fauna-print dressing gowns to every meal. Canadian Forces Joseph Belleville, whose tales of military camaraderie seemed homoerotic to everyone but himself. The mall walkers, the bridge enthusiasts, the cross-the-border day-tripping outlet shoppers. Sitting on park benches along the river, Gault and Aubrey enjoyed ridiculing all of their peers.

Although such a courtesy was unnecessary day after day, Gault always sought her permission before lighting a cigarette at one of their park benches. It surprised him to learn that she used to smoke herself.

"Didn't everyone?" she asked.

"You quit when?"

"Ages ago, before I married."

"Your husband didn't approve?"

Aubrey shrugged. "You know, once in a while, I still get a craving."

"Well," Gault said. "Far be it from me to tempt you, but I don't think you'll stunt your growth at this point."

"All right. Just one."

He hadn't lit a woman's cigarette in over a decade, but the act felt immediately familiar. A ridiculous and coy gesture, of course, but also intimate.

§

Her single cigarette became part of their daily ritual too. Only one, only on a park bench, and only after they had explored a new stretch of the path. Aubrey didn't want to fall into wicked ways, she explained.

One morning, after weeks of temperate late summer weather, rain splattered against the dining hall windows.

"Well, so much for our daily constitutional."

Except for the walking path, Gault and Aubrey hadn't yet gone anywhere together, and he meant to change that. His car, a full sized Buick Regal, had been sitting in the parking lot unmoved for nearly a month, and it was about time he took it on the road.

"Do you have any pressing errands we might run together?" he asked.

Aubrey shrugged. "A birthday card for my son-in-law. I've been thinking of a bird feeder for the balcony. Not exactly pressing."

"Hallmark and Home Depot."

"And I'd like to pick up something to read."

"Hallmark, Home Depot, and Chapters. We have our itinerary, madam. If we break for a coffee somewhere, we have a full morning ahead of us."

Their first stop was Home Depot, where they spent thirty minutes locating and selecting a miniature replica of a colonial manse.

"Virginia was right," Aubrey said. "No one gets out of that store quickly."

Stopped at a red light outside, Gault pointed out that three of the cars at the intersection were driving with expired plates.

"The white Civic, the white Voyageur, the grey Sentra."

Aubrey grinned at him. "Ever the police officer."

He shrugged. "Habit."

"Are you thinking of a citizen's arrest?"

He shrugged.

"So what is the most unpleasant assignment a police constable can receive? Cat trapped in a tree? Littering in a city park? Directing traffic in the rain?"

"Traffic accidents."

"I can imagine."

"The worst I ever saw was two families. Two couples in two minivans. Five children altogether. Only one father walked away."

Aubrey remained quiet, and he realized he'd changed the mood of their morning.

"Sorry," he said.

"Young children?"

"Yes."

"A terrible thing for you to see."

Her pity was genuine. He wondered how he might use it.

"No sense in dwelling." He shrugged.

On days that Virginia and Brie visited, Gault tended to stay in his suite with a book. Reading meant he ended up smoking more than he should, but the long stretches of time in an unpredictable criminal underworld were a good break from walks along the river. Consequently, the day he happened upon Aubrey and her daughter in the first floor corridor, he was at first put off. He'd only dashed out to steal a pastry from the dining hall.

"Good morning, Mrs. Moore."

The daughter was pushing the stroller, but Gault noticed that Brie wasn't in it. The little girl was gripping the side of the apparatus and waddling along.

"First steps this week," Aubrey said.

"Wonderful." He nodded. "Wonderful."

She introduced her daughter, who gave Gault a genuine smile as she put out her hand.

"Dr. Virginia Walters-Moore," he said.

She grinned again. The daughter, Gault thought, was very much like the mother. Both were won over with the smallest of attentions.

The introduction was followed by more gushing over Brie and her momentous walk—she'd certainly be a gymnast just like her cousins—and when conversation slowed, Aubrey invited him along to the dining hall for tea.

"I wouldn't want to intrude," he said.

"You wouldn't be an intrusion at all," Aubrey said.

The daughter was watching them talk, and Gault guessed Aubrey had mentioned him more than once.

"Well, in truth, I have a book waiting for me back in my room. I hope you understand."

"Of course," the daughter said. "My mother said you were a big reader."

It seemed Aubrey had more than mentioned him. Gault was further along than he'd expected; he and Aubrey had yet to embrace or kiss, and already the daughter knew small details about him.

"Retirement must be a wonderful time for all those great works of literature," the daughter said. "I have a long reading list in mind when I retire."

Though he felt the urge to laugh, Gault nodded and chanced a quick look at Aubrey. She was covering her mouth to hide a grin.

Gault eventually came to the conclusion that his sons were best estranged, and he decided the topic was best broached during a long contemplative walk along the river. It wasn't a matter to rush, of course, but he couldn't excuse Sam and Thomas's absences forever. The September weather was cooling, and Aubrey wore a light scarf at the neck of her cardigan. They would soon have to restrict themselves to short walks around Woodlawn's property, Gault supposed.

The park bench they stopped at today had an etched plaque embedded into one of its wooden slats. *Donated by Wilfred and Martha MacDonald.*

"That's sweet," Aubrey said.

"Yes." He passed her a cigarette and leaned forward to light it for her. The gesture had lost some of its playfulness, but it had become part of their routine, broken only when her daughter and granddaughter came to visit.

"So did Virginia wind up taking the extra year off?" he asked.

"Yes, she did. She doesn't want Brie in daycare just yet."

"Probably the right choice. It's good to have a career." He shrugged. "But once it ends, it ends. A child's resentment is forever."

"I notice your sons haven't visited."

There it was.

Gault shrugged. "They know I'm here if they need me." He let his voice trail off.

"But?"

"But they don't so much need me."

"Not sentimental about their father then?"

"Sentimental? No, they are not sentimental about me." He shrugged. "Perhaps they have reason, though. I was probably not the best of fathers. The job had a lot to do with it, I suppose."

Inventing a minimum of detail, he recounted how it wasn't always easy to be a police constable in the city—how he'd sometimes let himself get angrier than he should have, how he'd sometimes used slurs he shouldn't have, how he'd sometimes used more force than he should have.

"Do you remember that end-of-year demonstration at the college? It was in the paper. This would have been early eighties. Eighteen officers were suspended."

Aubrey did remember.

"I was one of the eighteen. Kept me from promotions."

Gault told her of other incidents. A traffic stop when he'd used an *insensitive epithet* on a guy who turned out to be a lawyer, a domestic disturbance when he'd overestimated the force of his club, an intoxicated transient he'd taken down when the man spit on him.

The job changed a person over time, he admitted.

"Yes," Aubrey nodded.

"I'm not making excuses."

"That's all right."

It was tiring to confess true failings aloud.

"And your sons?" she asked.

"Yes. It affected how they see me." He shrugged. "Right or wrong."

"Yes."

"Well, it all seems a long time ago now. No sense dwelling."

As he'd hoped, Aubrey's expression was more compassionate than critical.

"We should head back," he said, "if we want a good table for lunch."

"That's all right."

They sat in silence for a moment until Aubrey suggested they go out for lunch. Unfortunately, the restaurants around Woodlawn were typical suburban fare–Boston Pizza, Kelsey's, an East Side Mario's.

"Fast food with waiters," Gault said.

"Do you feel up to a drive downtown then?"

She was trying to cheer him up. A good sign, he thought.

"I'll have to skip my afternoon nap," he said.

Heading back down the path, they spent ten minutes learning that neither of them liked Chinese or Thai, but Indian was good if it wasn't too spicy. Conversation was remarkably easy between, Gault thought. He reached out and took her hand as they walked.

"Oh," Aubrey said. "This is a new development."

Gault nodded and opened his mouth to talk, but discovered that he couldn't. The pain in his head was quick, and he was unconscious before he hit the ground.

Why had they ever walked so far? Exercise was necessary at her age, of course, but why had they felt the need to wander such a distance from Woodlawn? That was what went through Aubrey's mind as she hurried back to the independent living home–that and the image of Gault's collapsed body, slumped over, half on the gravel path and half on the grass. His head had turned to the side and a small mouthful of vomit spilled onto his cheek and the ground beneath. Aubrey wished she could say that she sprinted back to Woodlawn and grabbed the maintenance fellow working on the shrubs in a matter of minutes, but she hadn't been able. She'd trotted as best she could, but winded, she was twice forced to a slow stagger.

"My friend has had an attack," she said. "On the path."

From that point on, events seemed to occur two and three steps ahead of her. The gardener fellow was inside calling emergency services before she even noticed that he'd dropped his hedge clippers to the lawn. Then, the fellow crossed back and ran past down the path. Should she follow him? Before realizing there was no sense in it, she was dragging herself up the path once again. Her body fought back and she watched as the gardener grew farther and farther ahead of her. Even a brisk walk was beyond her ability at this point. She heard but did not see the ambulance arriving, and by the time she returned to where Gault's body had fallen, it wasn't there. The ambulance had already departed, leaving ruts of exposed earth where it had driven off the road and onto the walking path. The gardener–Aubrey wished she knew his name–looked up at her as she approached. He was impossibly young, she remembered.

Younger than her children. There was alarm in his face, and he held his hand out as he came close to her.

"You must sit," he said.

A stroke. The general manager Ms. Sanderson did not think Aubrey should go to the emergency ward that morning, so she didn't. By the time a taxi cab took her to the city hospital the next day, Gault had been moved to a bed in the intensive care unit. He hadn't woken up, and Aubrey was able to learn that his heart seemed to have suffered some damage during the ordeal. The length of time between the incident and medical intervention was longer than the doctors would have liked. If he did recover, muscle control, speech, and mobility would likely not be what they had been.

As she wasn't family, Aubrey was not allowed to visit his bedside, and she spent much of that dismal afternoon alone in the ward waiting room. Though she tried to keep the image from her mind, what she kept picturing was how his wonderfully mischievous grin might now slope to the side—he would forever have that unhappy sagging smile she'd seen in stroke patients before. A telephone call to her daughter might have made Aubrey less gloomy, but she didn't feel up to explaining the situation to Virginia. A little before dinner hour, Ms. Sanderson passed by the waiting room and spotted her.

"You poor dear," she said.

Finished up for the day at Woodlawn, Sanderson had stopped in at the hospital to check in on Gault's condition before heading home. She had no idea Aubrey had been waiting here all day.

"Hanging around a hospital never did anyone any good."

In a scolding voice, Sanderson said she did not want to scold and managed to talk Aubrey into a tea downstairs in the hospital cafeteria. Two hours later, Gault's condition hadn't changed at all, and Aubrey accepted the woman's offer of a ride back to Woodlawn.

"We can come back together tomorrow," Sanderson said, "if need be." There was no need. He died in the night, and the general manager came to Aubrey's suite first thing in the morning with the news. Sanderson was needed at the hospital to clear up a few odds and ends, she said, but she didn't want Aubrey spending the day alone. Was there someone who could visit on a moment's notice? Aubrey told her not to worry and passed the morning in her housecoat, nodding off on the chesterfield twice before she returned to bed.

Over the next couple of days, Aubrey went out of her way to pass by Gault's suite on the first floor. The door remained closed, of course, and Aubrey imagined it would take a month or so to clear the place out. A month, at least. The sons would need a few days to arrange a funeral service, and they'd probably have to take time off work to sort through all those possessions. Thinking of those two sons, she tried not to grow angry, but such restraint was not easy. She couldn't help but imagine Sam and Thomas Junior casually boxing up their father's entire existence and hauling it off to the consignment shop down the road. Of course, they would hold onto a few keepsakes because this is what children do–photographs or maybe a memento from the police force–but would either of them be truly affected by the death? Would the sons turn sentimental toward their father after it was all too late? Aubrey decided she should let them know just how much their absence affected their father–these boys were due a reprimand and they should regret their actions.

Four days after Gault's death, she approached Sanderson to ask about the funeral arrangements, and the two women talked. At first, Aubrey couldn't make any sense of what the general manager had to tell her. Why would there be no funeral service? Why did Sanderson think Gault had been a lifelong bachelor and entirely childless? Surely, the woman was misinformed. Aubrey did not understand, but then, she did.

§

Although she wasn't entirely certain why, Aubrey decided not to tell Virginia of Gault's passing or of his many lies. Whatever Aubrey's reason—perhaps her bewilderment was too fresh, perhaps her gullibility was too embarrassing, or perhaps the wound was too private—she wasn't ready to discuss these matters with her own child just yet. Better to keep some thoughts to herself.

Fortunately, she didn't need to worry about revealing too much during this Saturday visit. Initially, Brie was fussy and didn't allow for much conversation, and once she was asleep, Virginia had news about her extended work leave.

"Paul and I decided that the best way to strike the right balance is for me to take the time off but also focus on a specific research project. This way, I'll be able to spend time as a mother without giving up my chances at tenure."

"That sounds good."

Aubrey nodded and looked at her granddaughter sleeping in the stroller.

"So we're interviewing for half-time nannies. Paul found this organization online and they match up nannies with two families. It works out for the nanny because she—or he, I suppose—isn't entirely dependent on one family for his or her livelihood, and it works out for professional parents like Paul and me."

"Yes."

Virginia had one hand on the side of the stroller, wobbling Brie rhythmically. Aubrey could remember doing this with each of her children when they were infants.

"One week, I'll be home with Brie Monday-Wednesday-Friday, and I can spend Tuesday-Thursday at the university library. And then the next week, the schedule flips. I'm home Tuesday-Thursday and at the library Monday-Wednesday-Friday."

"I see," Aubrey said.

"It should work out well."

Virginia took a sip from her tea and asked if something was wrong.

"On the tired side," Aubrey said. "That's all."

"I'm also looking into Baby Language Classes that Brie and I can do together. Maybe Spanish. I think it will be more rewarding than Mommy Massage."

"Yes."

Brie stirred in the stroller, and her head slumped to the side. Careful not to wake her, Aubrey adjusted one of the swaddling blankets and propped up the child's head.

"That's better," Aubrey said.

Her daughter again asked if there was something wrong, and Aubrey again said she was fine.

"A little preoccupied, I suppose." She shrugged. "My friend introduced me to his investment counsellor the other day." Aubrey hadn't planned on saying this, but she could tell her daughter was interested.

"Why?"

Aubrey shrugged again. "He has a few ideas about generating new income after retirement."

"Such as what?"

Her daughter was interested, Aubrey could tell.

"Overseas opportunities mostly."

"Is it wise to take chances with your savings? At this point?"

"It's just something I'm looking into."

It didn't take much to get her daughter's wheels turning, Aubrey saw. She could imagine Virginia relating this information to Paul as soon as she got home. Virginia might even get on the telephone to her brother and sister to discuss the matter.

Aubrey brushed her hand against her sleeping granddaughter's cheek. "She's such a sweet child."

SIX

In accordance with tradition, the six who will bear Tessa Powell (née Anderson) from the back of the Mason Funeral Services hearse to her Woodlawn burial plot are not immediate family, but men who have been selected for their indirect connection to the deceased; for the time being, Tessa Powell's lifelong friends, closest blood relations, and all sundry bereaved will stand aside and remain by the line of parked cars that leads from the south-east entrance to the graveyard. Long ago closed to new business, the Woodlawn cemetery most often now receives the survivors of husbands and wives who have already passed—widows and widowers who purchased twin plots and went on to endure after their spouse did not. Such is the case of Tessa Powell (née Anderson), beloved wife to the late Harold, loving mother to Sarah, dear mother-in-law to Edward, and cherished sister to the late Alice. Standing by the rear of the hearse, the six pallbearers that she named in her final requests wait while an attendant from the Mason Funeral Home unlatches the back gate, grasps a firm hold of a casket handle, and rolls the deceased smoothly outward. The attendant's movements are efficient, choreographed through years of repetition, and as he speaks, his words of instruction are clearly practiced. He addresses the six as *gentlemen* and explains that they are to lift the weight in unison and to follow the pace of the two men at the front. He points to their destination, the gravesite where a pastor already stands in wait and ready to deliver a final blessing, and in a calm, low voice, the attendant assures the six that he will follow them every step of the way. Purchased by Tessa and Harold Powell on credit some fifty years earlier and slowly paid off in installments, the gravesite is a twin plot some distance off. It is located in the much desired southeast corner of the cemetery, where wide maples provide visitors shade for hours of quiet reflection, and so the six will have to navigate carefully, travelling between narrow lines of elaborate graves while watching their steps to ensure that they do not traipse on another's hallowed ground. Making the noble journey from hearse to headstone even more precarious is the day's pathetic fallacy. After a night of steady drizzle, the sun rose to a heavy downpour that pounded the roof of the Mason Funeral Home throughout the memorial service, soaking the cemetery grass and creating a hazard that could slip up the funeral procession and spoil later memories of the ceremony. The six should, of course, be paying special attention as they walk, but they do not. In fact, as they move forward, their faces as blank as Stoics, the men bearing the maple casket polished to a gleam cannot stop their minds from wandering.

At the head of the coffin, Calvin Russell listens to funeral home attendant's instructions closely, making certain he lifts the weight of the casket uniformly and slowly. Because he is not related to the deceased, Cal was taken aback but pleased to discover his name mentioned in her final requests, and he wants to treat the role assigned to him with all appropriate solemnity. On the day that the estate lawyer contacted him, Tessa's neighbour in the Richmond Gates Apartments was, in fact, unaware of her passing, but he had been wondering why they hadn't bumped into one another for over a week. With eighteen floors and one hundred and eighty apartment units, Richmond Gates is not the kind of building that hosts holiday get-togethers in the lobby and does not have an organized tenant society, but for the past five years that he has occupied unit 1107, Cal has grown used to his conversations with his neighbour in unit 1103. These conversations began on the day that Cal moved in, after his childless marriage failed and he found himself not only alone, but isolated. What had happened to the handful of close friends he'd had all through high school and university? What had happened to his network of clients, coworkers, and companions at the office? Where was his family? Divorced at thirty, Cal found himself cut off from all community and connection. Consequently, when he noticed his elderly neighbour Tessa watching him through the eyehole in her door, he did not shake his head to himself and curse the snooping old bag, he did not avert his gaze and avoid eye contact with her in the mailroom, and he did not pretend he didn't see her when they bumped into one another in frozen foods at the IGA down the road. Instead, Cal made a conscious decision to smile genuinely when they walked into the elevator together and to thrust out his arm protectively and block the untrustworthy automatic door whenever they exited the elevator together. If he bumped into Tessa at the IGA—as often in produce as frozen foods, if truth be told—he asked about her day and offered to accompany her, helping her push her bundlebuggie across the intersection and back to the Richmond Gates. From these initial moments of contact, the two built an improbable friendship of sorts. Whenever Cal was finished with his *Newsweek,* he passed the issue along to Tessa; whenever she baked an almond orange cake for company, she set aside a bit for him. From short visits in her apartment, he observed a few peculiarities—her silver baby spoon collection from cities around the world and the sets of Windsor family dinner plates that lined the wall over the chesterfield—and he noticed a few undesirable traits—the ungenerous tone in her voice when she spoke of her daughter Sarah and the possibly racist remarks she made when speaking of the Vietnamese family in unit 1109—but most of what Cal knew of Tessa's life and the eight decades she lived were no more than biographical scraps picked up in passing conversation. She'd been in her apartment for over twenty years and before that owned a townhouse; she'd once had a husband, but he was gone long before she; the husband was a letter carrier and she worked in a post office behind the counter. Was that how they met? Cal didn't know, and now he never will. As the six begin their slow steps away from the hearse and southeast access road, Calvin Russell thinks he should have taken a spot in the middle of the casket. Unfamiliar with Woodlawn, he isn't entirely comfortable leading the way through the cemetery rows, but now that the six are moving forward, there is little he can do to stop them.

By unfortunate coincidence, the other man at the head of the casket is Vincent Mills, and like Cal, Vincent is entirely ignorant of the cemetery layout. Also like Cal, Vincent was surprised to be named as a pallbearer in Tessa's papers, for while he is the deceased's grandson, he is a relation only in name and by law. Before her death, Vincent had, in fact, met Tessa but twice: first at his father and stepmother's rehearsal dinner and then again at the wedding the following day. At the time of the nuptials, Vincent had recently graduated from school and had accepted an overseas teaching contract for two years in Seoul, which was followed by an eighteen-month position in Beijing and half a year of travel south through Jinan, Nanjing, Shanghai to Hangzhou. Homesickness and a lack of money brought him back to Toronto, where he has been staying temporarily on the foldout sofa of an ex-girlfriend and where he learned of his grandmother's passing. Thus, Vincent's memories of Tessa are few. For the rehearsal dinner, his father had booked a private room in a Keg in Richmond Hill, but the busy waitress attending to their party of twelve also had tables on the floor and the service was poor. One plate came with steak fries instead of garlic mashed, a prime rib was medium instead of medium rare, and coffee cups weren't refilled. Tessa's rib eye came covered in a slather of caramelized green peppers and onions, and although this side dish was fully described in the menu, and although Vincent's embarrassed soon-to-be stepmother Sarah tried unsuccessfully to silence his soon-to-be step-grandmother– *just scrap it off your goddamn plate*–the old woman refused to eat more than the baked potato that had come with the meal. At the wedding reception, Vincent and Tessa both sat at the head table, but on separate ends, and so they did not speak; he was, however, certain that he caught her rolling her eyes more than once during the after-dinner toasts. While Vincent's own opinion of his father's fourth marriage to a woman twenty years his junior was a near-complete indifference, the bride's mother clearly did not approve. During the short memorial service at the Mason Funeral Home, Vincent retraced his two memories of Tessa and thus exhausted his entire knowledge of her life. Had he been paying attention to the pastor leading the memorial, Vincent would have learned more, but his mind was then–as it is now–elsewhere. As he looks up over the headstones and sees the pastor waiting beneath the maples, Vincent thinks not of Tessa but of a cemetery he happened upon in Hangzhou, where the rows and columns of headstones were crowded tightly together. The grave markers were so close to one another, in fact, that at first, he did not understand how so many bodies could fit beneath the earth. Were the dead inserted vertically? Only later did he understand that under the ground were cremated fragments of ash and bone, compact inside their vessels. Strange to bury urns, he thought. Stranger still were the portrait photographs on each headstone. Transferred onto a white tile, black and white pictures were cemented above each deceased name. Some pictures showed healthy young faces and others withered and gaunt by age, but what struck Vincent was that the age of those in the portraits seemed to be in no way connected to the lifespan of the deceased, which meant that someone had made a conscious and considered decision when choosing just the right photograph. How would one decide the age of the photograph? How could one decide which age to remain for the decades, centuries, or millennia until the cemetery fell into complete ruin? Didn't such hope in a future after death make a joke of the years before death? Such pointless questions couldn't help but sadden Vincent. Suddenly feeling how alone and how far from home he was, he decided there and then to return to Canada, where he was in the process of reacclimating when his father contacted him about the news of Tessa's death. Walking through Woodlawn Cemetery past the many headstones, Vincent Mills cannot help thinking of the Hangzhou cemetery, and the pointless questions are once again troubling him.

Directly behind Vincent is the oldest of the six, and though he's positioned in the middle, Wilson Thatch does know where he is going. At one time, Wilson counted the deceased and the deceased's husband Harold as closest friends, and as such, Wilson was here in the Woodlawn Cemetery on the day of Harold's funeral and on many other days over the twenty years since. Sitting beside his dead friend's gravestone, the aging Wilson talked to Harold at length, apologizing for his betrayal of his friend and for his affection toward Tessa. Once upon a time, Wilson would have confidently said that he knew the deceased better than anyone else at her funeral—certainly better than any other of the six. Until the open casket viewing a few hours ago, however, he had not seen Tessa in over two decades, not since Harold's death, funeral, and burial. He had the pleasure and honour of carrying the casket on that day too, but at middle age, the task then was easier than it is now. With Harold's funeral over, Wilson and Tessa stood at the foot of the southeast entrance road, and holding her shoulders in his hands, he leaned forward to embrace her. What she told him then was that she didn't want to see him ever again. That was it. She banished him and he would never see her alive again. Wilson didn't argue at the time, for though he hoped such a punishment would not be coming, he had half expected it would, a comeuppance for his earlier misjudgment. How this resentment of some two decades began was a story that reached back even further in Wilson's memory, back to when he first moved to Toronto and started on at Canada Post. When he was first hired on and assigned to shadow Harold Powell, the older man had been working out of the Steeles and Yonge office for over a decade, walking a route that was no more than ten minutes from the front door of the townhouse where he and his wife Tessa were beginning their family. The delivery area meant lunches at home, and as Harold put it, it would have been downright inhospitable not to invite the new trainee along for soup and sandwiches. Their daughter Sarah was sitting in her highchair finishing up a purée that might have been prunes when the two of men walked in wearing their mail carrier uniforms, and the infant took an instant liking to Wilson, reaching her arms out and pleading to be held. He bounced the girl on his knee throughout lunch while her parents asked how he was finding the city, why he'd moved all the way down from Sault Ste Marie, and–*seeing as Sarah had taken such a shine to him*–if he'd like to come to Sunday dinner that weekend. They must have seen how alone he was, that's what Wilson figured. Though he liked riding the streetcar and seeing a new picture nearly every week, it wasn't easy alone living in a new city. The Powells became his first Toronto friends. Later, they invited him to come along to Ontario Place, which was just then opening up that summer, and then, because they hated to see him spend the holiday alone, they asked him over for Thanksgiving. By the time Wilson was assigned his own route, he was something of a fixture for Sunday dinners, and by the time young Sarah started into grammar school, he was something of an uncle to her. It wasn't until after the girl began secondary school that Tessa started at Canada Post and Wilson's brotherly feelings for her took on a different nature. More and more, women were leaving the house to work, so it only made sense that Tessa considered a job as her daughter needed her less, and when a counter position opened up at the Steeles and Yonge office, it again only made sense for Tessa to put her name in. The job meant Wilson saw even more of her, and often without Harold. Though Wilson hoped he would know better than to make a pass at her, he wasn't at all surprised when he did. They were in the back loading dock at the time, sorting parcels when he grabbed her shoulders and pressed himself against her. In his defense, she pressed herself against him as well, but that didn't make his actions any less wrong. There may have been some groping, and he may have opened a button on her Canada Post uniform as well, but they'd gotten so carried away that afterwards he wasn't certain what all had happened. Neither of them mentioned the incident when they saw each other for the following Sunday dinner or during any of the Sunday dinners in the years that followed, and the silence was a kind of punishment of its own, a decades-long penance for his misjudgment. At Harold's funeral, when she said she no longer wanted to see him, Wilson accepted the new punishment and hoped it would be the last, but it was not. She put his name in her final requests for a reason, Wilson knew. After another two decades, his comeuppance came again, and so while the physicality of a pallbearer's task should really have excused the seventy-three-year-old man, Wilson Thatch trudges along over the wet cemetery grass with rest of the six, glad that the formal pace is slow enough for him to keep up.

Like Wilson, middle-aged Henry Anderson too suffers from a debilitating guilt as he carries his Aunt Tessa forward through the wet cemetery and thinks of time spent with her years ago. As he was an older brother with a single mother, responsibilities fell to Henry early on: at seven years, he had to ensure his younger brother Elias wore a toque, mittens, or scarf before dropping him off at the babysitter's; at eight years, he had to teach Elias the proper way to make his bed, rinse his cereal bowl, and lock the apartment door before setting out for daycare every morning; and at nine years, he had to accompany young Elias on the TTC along Steeles to Willowdale Elementary before seeing him in at the junior kindergarten door. The many duties that their waitress mother had entrusted in him, of course, caused him more anxiety than was normal for someone so young, and the after-school hours he spent at Aunt Tessa and Uncle Harold's townhouse were a welcome relief. Two evenings a week, instead of returning to the depressing high-rise on Bathurst where they rented a small one-bedroom, Henry could forget about his brother and escape to the black-and-white television set in the townhouse basement for an hour of *That's Incredible* or *The Incredible Hulk,* though it was a drag that the Hulk always transformed into a sickly pale grey instead of the radioactive green he was supposed to be. Back upstairs for his favourite mushroom soup-tuna fish casserole, Aunt Tessa always made a fuss over Henry, astonished that he never needed extra hours of homework to get straight As on his report cards–*if only his cousin Sarah were so bright*–and she always sliced him an extra generous portion of almond orange cake, complimenting him for tending to Elias in a way that their careless mother, her own little sister Alice, never did. In his aunt's words, young Henry was *a person of substance.* She said he would go so far that he could become a doctor of surgery if that was what he so chose, and when she was old and grey, he could come by with his beautiful model wife in his limousine and give his Aunt Tessa rides all over the city.

And although Henry and Elias were both grown into adults when their mother died from the breast cancer that takes many middle-aged women, Tessa held Henry tightly as he cried at the funeral, patting his back again and again as one would a colicky child and repeating that he was *a person of substance*. In truth, she probably did not believe he would meet her limousine expectations, and as an adult, Henry can see that her words were intended only as kind encouragement for a fatherless boy. Still, between the person he once saw reflected in his aunt's eyes and the person he has grown into, there is such a disparity that Henry cannot help but feel disillusioned on the day of Tessa's funeral. A sales representative for the past twenty years, he has moved from the office equipment industry to the printing industry and back to office equipment, and though he has won a few in-house sales contests and he has single-handedly paid off nearly half the mortgage of his three-bedroom detached in Richmond Hill, he has never really distinguished himself in any way. Instead of a beautiful model wife, Henry went through a series of unwise girlfriends before settling into the on-again-off-again affair he's been having with a married accountant from payroll for eight years and counting. The relationship is, he of course knows, fundamentally wrong, but it does help to lessen his isolation. When his Uncle Harold died, Henry did try to absorb some of his aunt's sorrow, helping her move her belongings from the townhouse to the apartment and later visiting to hang her entire collection of royal family dinner plates according to her wishes, but the truth was that the Richmond Gates Apartments reminded him too much of the Bathurst rental where he'd spent his childhood, and so over the years, he stopped in less and less. At forty-five years of age, he sees that he is not at all a person of substance and that he was not a very good nephew, and the guilt he feels is twofold. Thus distracted, Henry Anderson has allowed his attention to drift, and on a hazardous patch of exposed mud underfoot, he loses his traction, momentarily altering the distribution of weight between the six pallbearers.

Fortunately, at forty-two, Elias Anderson is in better shape than his older brother. He's broad shouldered and physically powerful in a way that Henry has been jealous of for years, and even without thinking, Elias uses his strength to correct his brother's misstep, steadying the casket immediately so Henry can find his balance, and the procession can continue as if never disrupted. Like his brother's, Elias's own memories of his Aunt Tessa are also set in the deceased's townhouse on the two days a week they stayed after school, and while Elias did not descend to the basement for a relaxing hour of television, he also remembers that time fondly, but for entirely different reasons. Too young to be assigned homework of his own, Elias sat at the dining room with crayons while his older cousin Sarah completed her ninth grade assignments and the extra practice exercises her strict mother gave her. While Sarah cross-multiplied fractions and memorized provincial capitals, Elias worked through his stack of *Reading Rainbow, Great Space Coaster,* and *101 Dalmatians* colouring books. The last one was somewhat unsatisfying, he remembers, because for the most part, it featured black-and-white dogs that required very little colour, but that was all right because he actually spent much of his time at the dining room table sneaking glances of his older cousin. Sometimes, Sarah chewed on her bottom lip when puzzled by a long division problem. Sometimes, she stuck out her tongue while crosshatching the shading for an art class pen and ink sketch. And sometimes, she sucked on the ends of her long hair if bored with conjugating irregular French verbs. On days when he was lucky, Sarah would ask Elias for help; his tasks were limited to reading out from her French text so she could dictate new vocabulary words or following along in *the Merchant of Venice* while she recited a memorized passage. Even though he sometimes had to sound out words he wasn't yet old enough to read and he mispronounced lots of them, Elias could tell that Sarah liked his assistance. Her manner lightened when they worked together, and occasionally, she would even forget her mother's stern presence in the house and let out a loud laugh. At such times, their voices did draw Aunt Tessa to the dining room and she did silence them with a glare, but to Elias's way of thinking, his aunt's disapproval was worth the trouble. Back to his colouring, he would return to sneaking glances, and if Sarah caught him at it, he had a readied excuse and asked some question about the living room over her shoulder. How many silver baby spoons did Aunt Tessa have in her collection? Did Aunt Tessa let her watch the colour RCA in the living room or did she have to settle for the black-and-white downstairs? What did Aunt Tessa mean when she said that Sarah wasn't a person of substance? In later years, Elias grew not only to understand that Sarah had been aware of his crush all along, but also that Aunt Tessa had known of it as well, and instead of viewing his affection as the harmless phase that it turned out to be, she openly scowled at Elias. In his memory, his aunt scowled at much: at Sarah and him laughing in the living room, at having to cook extra portions of tuna fish casserole those two days a week, and at her own younger sister, Elias's mother. While Tessa's world view may have changed with the times enough to allow for a job out of the house, an unwed mother was still an unwed mother in her eyes, and an unwed mother with two sons from two fathers was a problem to hold her tongue about only sometimes. While she was not one to utter a profanity even in the darkest of moods, her less charitable descriptions for the boys' mother were *loose woman* and *harlot* and *waitress*. She seemed never to say such things around Henry, but for whatever reason, she let them slip in front of Elias, and even as a young boy, he understood that the words were a measure of how little she thought of him. This is what he remembered while the pastor delivered the memorial service in the Mason Funeral Home, and from where Elias was sitting, he sneaked glances of Sarah in the front pew. His hope was to catch her chewing on her bottom lip or sucking on the ends of her hair, but, of course, she wasn't. She was sitting uncomfortably next to her elderly husband and staring at the open casket, experiencing the confusing and conflicting sentiments everyone suffers through when a parent dies. Aunt Tessa had not been a big-hearted and gentle mother, Elias knew that much, but she had always been present, which was more than his own mother. On the other hand, Aunt Tessa was never able to display the tenderness or generosity of spirit that came to his mother easily. While he and Henry grew up in a rental apartment that could only be kindly called economical, Elias retains fond memories of that one-bedroom on Bathurst, and still today, he drives out of his way to pass by it whenever he can. Sometimes, when they were young and Henry fell asleep first, Elias sneaked out to the small living room to wait for his mother to return from a late restaurant shift, and she always let him curl up beside her in the foldout sofa bed. Although he may not be a person of substance, Elias knows that such beginnings were enough to propel him into a contented and well-adjusted adulthood: a stable carpentry job of twenty years, a steady wife of eighteen years, and a beautiful son of fifteen years. Elias has never suffered from the isolation that visits many, and he probably has his late mother to thank for that. Can Aunt Tessa say the same? Can her parenting skills be blamed for the alcohol troubles that Sarah had in her twenties, the string of men she had in her thirties, and her compromise of a marriage to a man some twenty years her senior? And, if this is the case, will Sarah eventually forgive any of her mother's trespasses? Elias Anderson didn't know, but stopping at the open burial plot to set down the casket, he hopes so.

Following the instructions of the funeral home attendant and the example of his father Elias, Daniel Anderson bends at the knees as he places the casket over the grave. Thick canvas straps attached to a metal frame of pulleys are stretched over the open hole, and though he tries not to, Daniel stares at the sight of the contraption. At fifteen years old, Daniel is experiencing his first death, so the proceedings contain a completely new brand of novelty. The charcoal grey suit he wears fits well enough but is loose in the shoulders because it is his father's, borrowed after they discovered that the navy blue sports coat Daniel wore to sophomore prom not three months ago was already too small. Shaking her head but with a smile, his mother swore that if he didn't stop growing, he'd be as massive as his father—*another great big brick shithouse,* she laughed. This sounded all right to Daniel, whose strongest connection in life is with his father. Unlike any of the other pallbearers, Daniel listened closely to the memorial service this morning, and though he could tell that—like himself—the pastor had never actually met his great Aunt Tessa, the sheer triviality of the biography was fascinating.

Before Tessa and her sister Alice were born, there was a brother who died from TB when he was only five. Her parents emigrated from Wales in the late thirties when she and her sister were just young girls, and before settling in Toronto, the family lived first in Halifax. Tessa excelled in school and graduated from junior college as a registered nurse's assistant, though she chose to raise a family and never worked in medicine. For her entire adult life, Tessa volunteered for the CNIB, first reading aloud to the blind and later stuffing envelopes for fundraisers. In her retirement, Tessa took up aqua fitness and swam five days a week.

Was this all that there was? At the end of his prepared notes, the pastor read a generic poem entitled "Do Not Stand at My Grave and Weep" and Daniel's attention drifted. At the graveside now, however, he is again intrigued; because they purchased a twin plot and a shared headstone, both Tessa Anderson's name and Harold Anderson's name are etched into the polished rock, but only his lifespan is recorded. Tessa's will be carved in shortly, Daniel assumes. Crouching down, the funeral home attendant releases the winches that hold the casket aboveground and the canvas straps slowly lower. At this moment, Daniel thinks of the finality of the event, of how Tessa Powell will be no more, and of the family members she has left behind, and like many at their first funeral, he imagines the death of his own loved ones. Some day he will attend his father's funeral, Daniel Anderson thinks sadly, and he will have to dress up in his own dark suit, and he will have to explain death to his own daughter or son.

With the canvas straps slack and the deceased beneath the ground, all of the six are all relieved to have carried out their obligations without incident. No one slipped on the wet grass and no one fell, thank goodness. Standing under the wide maples, the pastor will deliver a final blessing, and there may well be tears before the casket is covered in dirt, but the task assigned to them by the deceased's final requests is finished. Such is the end for Tessa Powell (née Anderson), neighbour to Calvin, grandmother to Vincent, friend to Wilson, aunt to Henry and Elias, and great aunt to Daniel. The casket is not, however, at rest. The rain that came down last night and through the morning has accumulated in Tessa's final resting place, leaving an oversized bath of muddy water in the hole, which each of the six lean forward to consider. The casket, a maple polished to a gleam, floats, of course, and as the six watch on, it is moving slowly across the surface of the brown water, knocking into the grave's interior walls and then changing direction until after a moment, it stops, adrift but motionless. Fortunately, none of the deceased's lifelong friends, closest blood relations, and sundry loved ones are present at the graveside to witness Tessa's final movements, and their future memories of the ceremony will not by spoiled by the sight that all of the six view with a sense of shame, their noble task suddenly and decidedly ignoble. For the Mason Funeral Home attendant, water in a grave is not uncommon, and he solves the problem as he has many times before, dragging over a heavy green tarp and drawing it atop of the hole.

THE VASECTOMY DOCTOR'S
ONLINE PRESENCE

Father of three, *Deaghan Potts* is an industrial architect and a twice-convicted impaired driver who lives at 781 Beaverwood Avenue in Manotick and whose LinkedIn resumé lists communication, administration, and synergistic negotiation as core career strengths. Childless widower *Deaghan Potts* is the cofounder and present secretary-treasurer of OCMRA, the Ottawa-Carleton Model Rocket Association, a non-profit organization for model spacecraft enthusiasts, and on his personal blog, he currently lists *The Ingenious Gentleman Don Quixote of La Mancha* as to-read in his sidebar bookshelf. *Deaghan Potts* is a Glebe United Church youth pastor, a Carleton University post-grad music therapy researcher, and a beloved husband, father, and grandfather who passed quietly during an afternoon nap in Orleans.

Not the Deaghan Potts you were looking for?

No, you can safely assume that none of these profiles is the *Deaghan Potts* you are looking for. Your *Deaghan Potts* is not an architect, not an enthusiast, not a pastor, not a post-grad, and definitely not deceased. The *Deaghan Potts* you are looking for is a vasectomy doctor–or euphemistically, a men's health specialist–and you are searching for information. You want to know what kind of man *Deaghan Potts* is, and you want to know before you schedule an appointment that will allow him to snip away at your vas deferens. Your GP scribbled down the name onto a note pad leaf, but you have little luck until you amend your Boolean and add an area code and telephone number. Then, the first, second, and third hits lead to the home page of *Dr. Deaghan Martin Potts* and *The Vasectomy Consultancy of Nepean*, where a slanting italicized script promises *a safe and expeditious scalpel-free procedure.* Scalpel-free? No, not really, but the incision is small. Quite small. Local anaesthetic. Back at work the next day. As your jolly red-faced GP explained, the phrase *scalpel-free* is less an accurate descriptor than a piece of convenient terminology to distinguish the technique from older, more invasive approaches. This was meant to be reassuring, you assume. What is less reassuring is the unimpressive website of Dr. Deaghan Martin Potts and the Vasectomy Consultancy of Nepean, which utilizes a MS *Civic* layout, a MS *Concourse* colour scheme and PowerPoint jpeg banner art. The design suggests that Potts chose to cut corners and costs by hiring a weekend web-developer instead of investing in and contracting a proper marketing professional. The resulting product does not inspire confidence.

Mediocre graphic design usually saddens you, and faced with such a reaction, you pause to consider the reasoning behind the feeling. Whether the advertising product is a xeroxed $3.00 coupon insert for a local pizzeria or clip art artwork on a self-produced compact disc of experimental jazz, poor commercial art and design strikes a note of hopelessness. In addition to sadness, the mediocre designs might, of course, equally inspire embarrassment or distain, but all of these reactions are perhaps tied to the same sense of hopelessness and futility: the majority of people do not and will never act upon artistic aspirations, and of the small vain minority that do and will, most fail. Such is human nature and such is the human condition. Better not to advertise at all than to give off such quiet desperation.

Nonetheless, the home page of Dr. D. M. Potts's Vasectomy Consultancy of Nepean offers four dropdown buttons underneath its title banner–*About, Contact, Location,* and *Media Highlights*–and the first of these options features an FAQ section with questions and answers useful and illuminating. Anaesthetics, recovery times, payment options, and provincial medical coverage information. Travelling farther down on the scroll bar, however, the FAQ grow increasingly unpredictable.

Will I still be able to exercise on a rowing machine?
Yes.
Will I have to wear boxer briefs instead of jockeys?
No.
Will there be any scarring on the scrotum?
Minimal.

You must wonder what sort of vanity inspired the last of these questions. At the bottommost of the page, the FAQ links to *Biographical Information* that explains Dr. Potts's professional career in a single paragraph.

Born and educated in Kingston, Dr. Potts studied Biology as an undergraduate at Queen's University, where he graduated from medical school and later returned for a specialization in urology. After a successful decade at the Ottawa Renal Clinic of the Westboro Hospital and a year with Men's Health Partners of South Nepean, Dr. Potts opened the Vasectomy Consultancy of Nepean, which is now entering its fifth year of operation. He is married with seven daughters.

Beside the paragraph is a black and white headshot in which a late-forties-early-fifties Potts looks at the camera from behind an aggressively stylish pair of glasses, a design that only architects, jazz musicians, and small gallery owners can really pull off well. The photograph was taken at a slightly downward angle, making you wonder if Potts isn't attempting to hide a growing second chin, a problem common enough in men of a certain age. Perhaps Potts tilts his head downward for all photos and has even taken to angling his head in this manner while shaving in the bathroom mirror. Perhaps vanity has made a ruin of Potts's self image and changed it to a self-delusion—yet another problem common in men of a certain age.

Urology seems like such an unlikely specialty for someone to choose, and you can imagine that Potts at one point may have looked toward other, more glamorous specialties–something noble like neurosurgery. And if, like all professions, medical doctors operate within an unspoken social hierarchy, are urologists near the bottom of that pecking order? Keeping low company with chiropodists and gastroenterologists? And perhaps the situation is even worse for the pitiable Potts. Doctors often marry doctors and children of doctors often become doctors; Potts's immediate and extended family and social circle may well contain sports medicine surgeons, paediatric oncologists, and research geneticists. Do they look down upon your prospective vasectomy doctor? Is he mocked behind his back at medical conventions? Do the in-laws let unkind remarks slip at family Thanksgivings and Christmases after one too many drinks?

The doctor's single year between the renal clinic and his own consultancy firm is curious, and a quick Google search shows that the Men's Health Partners of South Nepean is no longer open. The defunct partnership's website, however, remains in partial operation, forgotten online detritus floating about like a broken-off piece of Sputnik in the outer-most atmosphere. Many of the links are dead.

The page you are looking for could not be found.

You do learn that the onetime partnership between Dr. Deaghan Martin Potts and Dr. Danton Robison offered treatments for erectile dysfunction as well as scalpel-free vasectomies, and while this short-lived partnership may have ended for any number of reasons, two causes are the most likely candidates:

1) Potts and Robison were once friends but no longer are–they had a personal falling-out serious enough to close the professional partnership down.

2) Or, more likely, Potts struck out on his own because The Vasectomy Consultancy of Nepean is a private practice and better

THE VASECTOMY DOCTOR'S ONLINE PRESENCE

business model. Treatments for a complex range of problems like erectile dysfunction would be hopelessly convoluted and involve any number of physiological, psychological, and pharmacological components. Too much overhead. Better to follow the examples of KFC and Subway and focus on vasectomies as a single menu item. Located in an affluent and growing family city with a large population of government employees who enjoy full medical coverage, a private vasectomy business is sure to flourish, and the operating costs would be very little. A few examination rooms, malpractice insurance, someone to answer the phone, and Bob is your uncle.

Google Earth confirms the good doctor's business savvy, for the business address of the Vasectomy Consultancy of Nepean is also a residential address: an early-century colonial with three floors and what looks like about 3000 square feet. The website's 360-degree photograph feature reveals that the building has a separate side entranceway, over which hangs a sign painted in white and green. The print on the sign has been blurred out by pixels, but this entryway must be a business entrance separated from Potts's own living quarters. Potts lives and works in one location, home and home page; the setup is ideal, the stuff of tax accountants' dreams. At such financial acumen, you cannot help but be impressed.

Fourteen ratings for Potts are posted on *ratemydoctor.ca,* and they are all quite old, all of them listing the Westboro Hospital under the *Institution* heading. As urologist at the Renal Clinic in the hospital, Potts enjoyed an overall 4.4 approval on a 5.0 scale, and the ranking would have been close to perfect if not for a single patient named *Johnr57.*

Staff: 0
Punctual: 0
Knowledgeable: 1
Helpful: 0

Overall Rating: 0.25

Potts is a d*Ck who thinks his better then his patients Made me wait 30 min. and spoke down to me, Seems insecure if you ask me.

The *Knowledgeable: 1* rating is curious. Why not zeros across the board?

You can safely suppose that Potts has visited this site himself and has read through all fourteen of his own ratings. Further, it isn't hard to imagine that a vain man like Potts would want to dismiss *Johnr57* as an ungrateful and ignorant crank, the kind of time-waster would post a three-star rating of *The Ingenious Gentleman Don Quixote of La Mancha* on Amazon.ca and resolutely believe his opinion valid. However, Potts would not likely shake off the *Overall Rating* of *0.25* quite so easily, for even the vain are brought down by human nature, human nature focuses on the single negative, forgetting and deemphasizing the significance and gratitude of the thirteen positives. A small part of Potts would recognize the legitimacy in *Johnr57*'s claim.

Your heart goes out.

After Google, Bing produces mostly repeat results, but you are also taken down an unexpected path–to jazz pianist *D. M. Potts.* Further varied searches reveal that there is a *D. Potts* who plays monthly shows at a piano bar in Westboro; he has self-produced one solo compact disc of Gershwin covers, and he plays in a three-piece jazz band known as *Medical Music.* The coincidence is too much. The band's poorly designed website, *The Medical Music Trio,* contains istock photos of smoky bars and sax, drums, and a piano, but no pictures of the members themselves; the *Schedule* button, however, reveals that the three musicians play a twice-monthly gig at a supper club in Cornwall, and on the supper club's website, a photograph of the band is included under the *Special Events* tab. The guitarist and bassist are pictured in the foreground of the photograph, and behind them is your own Dr. Deaghan Martin Potts, angled so his piano bench faces the camera, an elbow rested on the edge of the keys and his head tilted forward to hide extra chin. With his body slouched on the piano bench, there is no way for him to hide his middle-age belly, which pulls at the lower buttons of his white linen shirt.

At such a sight, you cannot help but be filled with an ambivalence containing sadness, embarrassment, and distain. The supper club photograph cannot be taken as anything but concrete evidence of unfulfilled aspirations; while financially successful in his chosen career, this man of a certain age has revealed himself to be among the small vain minority who have tried and failed. You can imagine that jazz piano has been a long-time dream, starting in childhood when Mom and Dad Potts paid for Monday, Wednesday, Friday lessons. The teenage DM Potts studied every Saturday and Sunday with a private piano teacher and rushed home at the end of every school day to practise, practise, practise, and at Queen's, the undergraduate Potts booked a session room in the music therapy department in between required lectures and labs every chance he got. His Biology major began a self-compromise, a subject he happened to pick up easily while he spent his weekends rehearsing and playing any venue in Kingston that would have him. Over time, however, school and studies demanded more of his attentions, until one day, he was submitting the bulky manila envelopes that contained his medical school applications, and he had to pause at the mailbox to realize he hadn't sat down at a piano in over two months' time.

Maybe this is not the man you want performing a delicate, life-altering procedure upon your life-giving delicates.

In a more derisive mood, you might imagine *ratemymiddleage. ca* and the ranking for Deaghan M Potts and The Medical Music Trio on such a site.

Feasibility of Aspiration: 0
Advisability of Aspiration: 0
Freedom to Pursue Aspiration: 1
Self-Awareness Demonstrated by Aspiration: 0
Overall Rating: 0.25

But thoughts of this kind are unkind. Such aspirations in middle age are at once pitiable and admirable, and while distain is both appealing and easy, such an attitude is hard to sustain, for you too will eventually be of a certain age. You too will come to an age when you are beyond tilting at windmills. You have already come to an age at which more children no longer seem like a wise option. You cannot help but be filled with ambivalence and quiet desperation, but you decide to go ahead and book an appointment with Potts.

REMEMBER THE LLAMA

Act One

Neither Colin Kapelovitz nor Sarah Phillips knew the deceased well. Colin had met Mrs. Rosetta Johnson only once–on a Sunday afternoon when he accompanied his elderly mother to the annual Family Day event hosted by the IGA where she worked a cash register. Family Day that year was a picnic affair, attended mostly by younger employees with little children, but Colin got to meet many of his mother's coworkers, and in all, he was glad he'd attended. His mother had taken the part-time cashier position after his father passed. She worked not for the money, but because, in her own words, she needed to push herself out of the apartment above the family store and into the world of people. Once, long ago, she'd spent her days in the family hardware alongside her husband, and Colin had insisted that she was more than welcome to return anytime she wanted. Though he was manager and ran the entire business, it was still technically her store. Both of them knew such an arrangement wouldn't work, though, and he was relieved when she took the IGA job. On Family Day, she introduced him around the picnic tables full of her many smiling coworkers from the bakery, deli, and produce departments–including Mrs. Rosetta Johnson from payroll–and it seemed to him that his mother's plan had worked. She'd gotten herself out of the apartment and into the world of people. That was five years before Rosetta Johnson's funeral. In that time, his mother's hands had grown too much of a bother to work the register, and she'd had to give up her three shifts a week, leaving her with fewer and fewer social outings. Colin believed far too many of these outings were funeral services of friends and acquaintances and people she knew once upon a time back when, and he also believed that such functions should not be attended alone. And so, when Colin could, he had the assistant manager take over the store and he accompanied his mother.

Sarah was somewhat more familiar with Mrs. Rosetta Johnson than Colin, but not by any significant margin. As members of the seven-member Bathurst Towers tenant association, Sarah and the deceased had assembled in the building's conference and party room whenever a new resident application was submitted for review. Because the desirable building was within walking distance to a TTC transfer stop, an IGA, and an indoor shopping centre, the rental units in Bathurst Towers did not open all too often. In fact, vacancies in the building occurred most frequently as the elderly tenants aged and died of natural causes well into the restful autumns of their lives. As the youngest member of the association by a good twenty years, Sarah knew she'd been asked to join only because of her perceived knowledge of the law. Everyone in the building knew she'd completed two years of law school at Osgoode, everyone knew she'd taken a year off to work the reception desk at a law firm, and everyone knew she would eventually graduate and go onto articling once she saved the tuition money. What no one on the tenant association seemed to understand was that she knew next to nothing about tenant and landlord rights. Nonetheless, the association was an easy way for Sarah to get to know her neighbours, and it was the one openly impractical pursuit in her otherwise overly practical routine. Meetings with the elderly association members included butter tarts and finger sandwiches, and the conversation was as much chitchat as business. If not for Mrs. Rosetta Johnson, the application reviews might well have been indistinguishable from any of the building's potlucks. For Rosetta, the association meetings were an opportunity to voice her many complaints against Bathurst Towers. Residents too often left the laundry room in a horrid mess. The hallway corridors were seldom vacuumed on schedule. The *Globe and Mail* went missing from her doorstep at least once a week. Rosetta–and never *Rose*–also made the proceedings unpleasant because she was one of those people who believed in the rightness and goodness of procedure above all else. Every meeting included documented minutes and every motion had to be seconded and thirded before approved and recorded. The woman had been exhausting. When she died, though, the tenant association all agreed that not sending a representative from Bathurst Towers to the funeral would have been unkind. Even the petty warrant tribute.

Held in the McAllister Funeral Home, the services for Ms. Rosetta Johnson included a two-hour open casket visitation and a memorial ceremony led by Reverend Robert O. Reid to be followed by the cemetery interment and a luncheon at the home of niece Gladys Tennant. Though Colin and Sarah had not yet met and neither one of them would voice such an opinion, they both independently thought that the services were excessive. There were less than two dozen mourners present that day, after all. Wasn't such a small turnout dispiriting enough without prolonging the matter? During the visitation, the lid of the casket stood open in McAllister's smaller viewing room, the deceased's three commemorative wreaths filled out by the funeral home's own bouquets and all arranged tastefully around an easel supporting a framed portrait of the deceased. The photograph looked professional, and in it, a much younger Rosetta Johnson smiled with her chin tilted upward, her expression not yet hardened and her brunette hair not yet faded to white. It would have been taken in her early thirties, Sarah guessed–at a time when the two of them would have been peers. The hopeful look in the photo troubled Sarah. What possible damage could have turned that happy young lady into the persnickety woman Sarah knew from the tenant association? Was this change the consequence of a particular calamity or a protracted series of disappointments stretched out over a lifetime? Colin's thoughts upon seeing the portrait were less reflective. He wondered why anyone would place an air-brushed and decades-old studio portrait next to an open casket. Was not this the most morbid kind of before-and-after imaginable?

Afterwards, in the smaller west chapel of the McAllister Funeral Home, Reverend Reid spoke from prepared notes, weaving the summary of a lifetime with eulogy, homily, and an ill-chosen biblical reading. Instead of the more common epitaph chestnuts from the Gospels, Reid selected Balaam and the donkey to accompany the standard Psalm 118. He explained how the Lord allowed the donkey to see an angel unseen by Balaam, how Balaam beat the donkey, and how the Lord interceded to grant the animal voice. Unfortunately, the point of the story was unclear. It seemed to have something to do with the unconditional kindness owed to even lesser creatures or something to do with the unexpected worth of lesser creatures or some such thing. Neither Colin nor Sarah was sure.

Sarah might have skipped out on the graveside ceremonies, but *in for a penny, in for a pound* was in her nature, the unspoken watchwords of her thirty years, and so she joined the row of cars behind the hearse. Over the following week and for the decades of marriage and shared parenthood until Colin's death at fifty-eight, Sarah would many times think that her stubborn tendency had served her well on the day of Rosetta Johnson's funeral, for if not present at the graveside, she would not have misread the trouble in Colin's forlorn and faraway expression and she would not have approached him.

The truth was, however, that Colin was not at all troubled at that particular moment. He was puzzled. Standing at the graveside, he was puzzled by the notion that a funeral attended by few mourners was somehow lesser than one with rows and rows of packed pews, and the further implications of the assumption. Did it mean that one deceased person's life was somehow lesser than another's? A small funeral meant a small person and a large funeral meant a big person? That could not be so, and yet it seemed to Colin that the misconception was widespread. A decade earlier, at his own father's crowded funeral, the rabbi had claimed that the sheer number of mourners present was a testament to the quality of the deceased's character. *The many lives of those that he touched.* At Rosetta Johnson's graveside, Colin looked forlorn and faraway at that particular moment because he had just concluded that the phrase was meaningless.

"You seem troubled?" Sarah placed a hand on his arm.

From the sympathy in her voice and the crease of her brow, Colin right away understood her misunderstanding, and he wanted to tell her that he was fine. He wanted to explain that he didn't even really know Mrs. Rosetta Johnson and he wasn't in any way bothered or affected by her death. Fortunately, he did not say any of these things. Instead, he nodded and in a low voice told Sarah that she was kind to ask.

Three days later, in bed for the second night in a row, Colin and Sarah replayed their first words to one another, reconstructed their first impressions of one another, and allowed themselves to laugh. Colin told her that her concern seemed so genuine that he just couldn't tell her the truth. Sarah told him that his face seemed so pained and so serious that she thought he was just barely holding up. Other pillow talk observations of their first meeting came later in the week. Sarah had noticed he let his mother hold his arm throughout the service, but he didn't hover around her during the visitation or the luncheon. Colin had noticed that she attended the service unaccompanied and that her calves looked especially striking in black stockings. Months into their relationship, Sarah admitted that she had already planned on offering up her telephone number before the luncheon where they lined up together at the coffee urn. Colin admitted that he didn't drink coffee.

"Such inappropriate behaviour for a funeral," she said.

Although they were then into their thirties and had been adolescents during a decade of supposed freedoms, their total combined number of lovers at the time of meeting was five. During university, she'd dated a man from Intro to Political Science for three years, and in law school, she had successive relationships with men from Torts, Contracts II, and Property. Through high school and most of his twenties, Colin had dated and been engaged to the same woman, who had belatedly realized that he possessed no great ambitions beyond running his inherited hardware store and who quickly broke off the engagement. Neither Sarah nor Colin possessed adventurous histories. No casual partners, no one-night stands, and before one another, no sex on a first date. As a result, they could not help but feel somewhat embarrassed by their sudden and mutual attraction.

Though ashamed to be thinking such thoughts, Colin was the rejected fiancé of a protracted engagement, and he asked himself if he wasn't rebounding. Should he really commit to someone he'd known less than a year? Wouldn't she tire of him eventually? Though ashamed to be thinking such thoughts, Sarah was the daughter of two lawyers and naturally asked herself if she wasn't settling for a man with little to no education. Should she really give up her search for an equal partner? Wouldn't she tire of him eventually? Such second guessing was natural, of course, and in the end, mattered little. What mattered to her was that he was the kind of man who carried his parents' wedding picture in his wallet, and what mattered to him was that she was the kind of woman who refused to ask her cold parents to help her out with law school tuition. What mattered was how easily they talked in bed.

"There is the problem of how we met," she said.

"Yes."

She was curled into him, under his arm, and they could not see one another's expressions. Their voices were playful, though, and both guessed that the other was grinning.

"Do we tell people we met a funeral?"

"A bit morbid."

"Worse than a drunken meeting at a bar?"

"Worse than a desperate meeting through classified ads?"

"We could just be evasive."

"Yes."

"Or we could lie."

"I say we lie."

"We could just make something up and lie."

"How did we meet?"

"How we met? Oh, that's an interesting story."

Interlude A

How they met was an interesting story. They both worked at IGA throughout high school. She was a cashier and he was a stock boy, and though they'd been there since freshman year, their paths never crossed, their shifts never overlapped, and they did not meet until senior year. The sad truth was that cashiers and stock boys moved in very different social circles, for as in every other workplace, the employees at IGA were subject to a strict, though unspoken social hierarchy. The chances of a cashier and a stock boy dating were as slim as a fishmonger befriending a green grocer. The one time that the impossible barriers between castes disappeared was at the annual Family Day picnic, where butcher and baker could lower their defenses and enjoy an afternoon feast of potato, bean, and fruit salads. On this day, she signed up for the wheelbarrow race but lacked a partner, and on this day, he signed up for the three-legged race but lacked a partner. In a way, their meeting was inevitable, and as the sun set on Family Day, the cashier and the stock boy sat across from one another on a picnic bench.

Interlude B

How they met was an interesting story. Their apartments at the Bathurst Towers weren't exactly across the hall from one another–she was in 13G and he was in 13B–but she passed by his door three or four times every day to get to the elevators, and he passed by her door every three of four days to get to the garbage chute. In spite of this close, close proximity, however, they never once made elevator small talk on their way down to their workaday worlds, and they never once awkwardly spied one another in their pajamas and bathrobes while retrieving their weekend *Globe and Mail* from the hallway. As happenstance had it, they'd once spent thirty minutes together in the main floor laundry room–her dryer load of towels overlapping his washer load of colour cottons–but on that particular day, she was absorbed by landlord and tenant case law and he was absorbed by a trade catalogue of new riding lawnmowers, and consequently, the opportunity for them to meet and fall in love passed unnoticed. They would not meet for another two years, not until the Bathurst Towers holiday potluck, where they both at once reached for the last butter tart on the tray. Laughing, he apologized and said she should have it. Flirting, she laughed and said she should have it.

Interlude C

How they met was an interesting story. Balaam's Donkey was not the kind of memorable zoo where families could pass an entire day touring pavilions of species organized by continent and habitat, but it was clean and kept up well enough. It was exactly the kind of economical petting zoo where she could take her niece and he could take his nephew for a pleasant afternoon. What her niece liked best was the overcrowded bunny hutch, where there always seemed to be a brand new litter of dwarf rabbits darting about and the oversized mother rabbit always allowed herself to be petted. What his nephew liked best was the camel, which could be ridden for two dollars on top of the door charge and which, from time to time, coughed out awful mouthfuls of crusty sputum. Such manners appealed to the nephew's sense of humour, and it wasn't fair to blame the camel for being a camel. The eponymous donkey inhabited the petting zoo's central pen, fenced in with a crowd of sheep, goats, llamas, and alpacas so placid that they barely reacted when timid children reached out to pet them. The niece and the nephew both adored standing in amongst the animals, and all Sarah and Colin had to do was stand back and marvel at the scene. It was while watching the children interact with the sheep and goats that she first noticed him, and it was the troubled look on his face that caused her to approach. As it turned out, Colin was not at that particular moment troubled at all, but he was puzzled. He was trying to remember the difference between llamas and alpacas. He was fairly sure that the llama was the taller animal and the alpaca was the shorter, but he could not be entirely certain. While many men might have suppressed such uncertainties in themselves, the unspoken watchwords that nagged at Colin's nature were *what you don't know could fill volumes,* and he realized that he could not even say which geographic region–neither country nor continent–each animal was native to. It was like the names of constellations and species of butterflies and subgenres of twentieth century jazz, he concluded; there was much that he knew he knew nothing about.

In the main pen at Balaam's Donkey, Colin looked forlorn and faraway because he had just concluded that no matter how much one knew, there would always be infinitely more that one knew one knew nothing about.

"You seem troubled?" Sarah placed a hand on his arm.

Act Two

From time to time, in the early years of their marriage, Colin and Sarah referred to all three of the stories they invented that night. Repainting the master bedroom after she moved into his apartment, she remarked that it was encouraging to see a stock boy and cashier working together so very cooperatively. On their first wedding anniversary, he purchased a bouquet of lilies to go along with a lacquered jewelry box he made by hand, and on the small card tucked amongst the blossoms, he wrote *from the boy in 13B to the girl in 13G*. In the parking lot outside BallyCliffe, the assisted living home he moved his mother into after her second stroke, she kissed his forlorn and faraway eyes and told him he seemed troubled.

"I am," he said.

For whatever reason, the story that endured was Balaam's Donkey. Over time, the exact details of their fiction faded. Did he have a niece and she a nephew, or was it the other way round? It didn't matter. The pleasure they had felt while building the stories did not fade, and recalling that night, they would both feel it all over again. It was a playful and warm pleasure, a collaboration they shared as they smiled at one another's suggestions and added to one another's ideas, and eventually, all that feeling was distilled down to the phrase *remember the llama*. During the many hours of review before her Constitutional Issues II examination, he quizzed her from her pages and pages of study notes, but occasionally he stopped to calm her anxiety. *Remember the llama*, he asked as if he were the silliest of tenured professors. At the door of their town-house, greeting their first ever pack of trick-or-treaters, he grinned and pointed out the two kids in the camel costume. *Remember the llama,* he asked as if tickling her in the ribs. The week after her first miscarriage, standing next to her at the sink, he set down his dish towel and put a hand on her shoulder, ending the stalemate of sad quiet that had stretched for days. *Remember the llama,* he said as if beseeching her to keep faith. In the shorthand language of their long marriage, these watchwords came to mean a great number of things and carried Sarah and Colin through their worst troubles and best joys.

If asked about the couple's worst troubles, Sarah would have said they had more than a fair share. Because their courtship had occurred in something of a flurry—they'd moved in together, discussed marriage and married in less than a year—Sarah applied to defer her already-postponed third year of law school, and when she did return, too much time had passed. By the end of her first semester back, she was on academic probation, and by the end of the second, she more or less stopped struggling altogether. It made no sense to waste any more money on tuition. The logical compromise was a career as a paralegal, and after a quickie six-month college certificate, she found a firm within walking distance to their new townhouse. The firm primarily employed non-union contract paralegals on an hourly wage—not an ideal situation—but permanent union positions were all internal, and Sarah decided on patience. With the economy what it was, few places were hiring, and with two years of law school, she was overqualified. If she put in the time, Sarah reasoned, she would soon be paid a livable salary. This did not happen.

If asked about the couple's worst troubles, Colin would have shrugged. Everyone has troubles, he would not have said. While the hardware store was never exactly a prosperous endeavour, it had been profitable–profitable enough for his parents to raise him and pay four employees a livable salary with a modest benefits package–and Colin worked hard to ensure that the business did not fall into decline after his father's passing. He had a wife and a mother to worry about, after all, and for much of her old age, his mother needed that apartment upstairs. Consequently, when the store stayed afloat, Colin couldn't help but feel gratified, and when the store expanded, he couldn't help but feel proud. The expansions were never exactly bold–a new sign above the window front, an elevated display for each year's new mower models–but he believed that these small improvements would help. Even with the economy what it was, Colin thought he could stay put and compete with the larger box stores that were opening more and more on the fringes of the city. This did not happen.

By the time Sarah was offered a permanent position, she had turned fifty-four and bitter. How could she not? Like most of her generation, she'd been raised to believe in the preeminence of a university education, and after six years in school, she had the status and salary of an office clerk. Every day for twenty years, she dressed in business professional, but never once for twenty years was she paid a business professional salary. How could she not turn her disappointment inward against herself and outward against her husband? How could the topic not come up during the quarrels every marriage must endure? How could she not from time to time wonder what might have happened had they never married?

By the time his mother was moved from the apartment above the store and into BallyCliffe, Colin had been forced to lay off two employees. The two that remained had worked in the hardware store so long that they had known his father. Compared to letting them go, it was better to sell and make what small profit he still could. He'd run the store for nearly thirty years, and though it had been a good run, how could he not feel that he'd let his father down? At fifty, Colin took an assistant manager position in the garden centre of a Home Depot. Hauling skids of manure sacks and stocking ceiling high shelves with decorative clay pots for hours and days at a time, how could he not feel defeated? How could he not feel that his wife's bitterness was deserved? How could he not from time to time wonder if she wouldn't have been better off without him?

If asked about their greatest joys, Sarah and Colin would have grinned in unspoken agreement. Hannah.

Because the couple didn't marry until their thirties, they were off to a late start and much was on their plate already–she had a career to get going and he had a store to keep going. When the question of children came up, they postponed, and later, biology refused to cooperate. Nearing forty, Sarah was convinced they would never conceive and become parents. In defeat, Colin too had come to feel this way, but he would never admit it aloud. They were wrong. Hannah was born, and like all new parents, they could hardly believe their own hearts' emotions.

"It just flattens you," he said.

"It does."

Asleep in their bed, Hannah lay on her side between Colin and Sarah. The couple was curled in around her, grinning at the expression on their child's face.

"I could just stare at her for hours."

"Your heart grows three times its normal size."

"Like the Grinch after he stole Christmas."

"Or like high school infatuation. Uncomplicated and constant."

"Yeah. I can't quite believe anyone else has ever felt this same way."

"I can't believe I'll ever feel any differently."

"I hope it doesn't become too complicated."

"The feeling?"

"It will change. Over time, will it change? I hope it doesn't change."

"Me too."

Act Three

Her parents' uncomplicated tenderness did change over time, of course, but not by much, and this was, Hannah knew, the advantage of older parents. Her father never took her to work and stuck her at an empty desk with a colouring book; he sat with her for hours at a time sorting a pile of nuts and bolts and when she grew bored of it, he read her as many storybooks as she wanted as many times as she asked. Her mother never hurried her through the junior kindergarten door and grew impatient if Hannah took too long changing from her outdoor shoes to indoor shoes. Her mother stood outside the junior kindergarten window waving and blowing kisses until the teacher said the class had to sit down for circle time. And although Hannah wouldn't be able to name her parents' strategy of positive reinforcement for many years more, she always sensed that their daily flattery must have been deliberate and planned. *You're clever at brushing your teeth because you're coordinated and thorough, you always win at ISpy because you're attentive and observant, you always remember spelling vocabulary because you're conscientious and careful.* Even through the adolescent years when most mothers' and fathers' thoughts toward their children become too complicated to express, they adored her without reservation. At fourteen, when she pierced her lip with a silver bolt, her father told her it looked as cute as a button, and at fifteen, when she dyed purple streaks into her hair, her mother told her they complemented her natural colour well.

The disadvantage of older parents was, Hannah discovered, that sometimes they died early. A month before her eighteenth birthday, her father had a heart attack. He might have survived, but at the time of the incident, he was at the top of a ladder straightening a new shipment of eaves troughs. Together, the head injury and the heart attack meant that he died in the back of the ambulance before he ever made it to emergency. The hospital wound up delivering his body to the funeral home before Hannah and her mother had a chance to see it. All that they got at the hospital was a plastic Ziploc bag containing his personal effects.

The funeral was not well attended. A few people from the Home Depot came. A handful of distantly removed cousins came. A caregiver from BallyCliffe wheeled Hannah's grandmother in. The turnout did not bother Hannah, however. If, as the saying went, funerals were not for the deceased but for the living, then a small, quiet service was fine for her. Afterwards, back at the townhouse, her mother went upstairs for a rest and Hannah sat at the kitchen table with a tea. She was holding the mug and waiting for it to cool when she spotted the plastic bag containing her father's things on top of the refrigerator, where it had been sitting since the day of the heart attack. She sipped from her mug and imagined her and her mother going through his leftover possessions over the next few weeks and months. The clothes from his side of the master bedroom closet. The jewelry box that contained old watches and silver dollars. The boxes of mementoes from the old hardware store.

Hannah stood and retrieved the plastic bag from the top of the refrigerator. Inside, she found her father's house and car keys attached to a ring she'd made him nearly a decade earlier at summer swim camp. Predictably, his wallet held photographs of her and her mother, some of which Hannah had seen, but a few that she hadn't. Hannah in her first softball uniform. A cat named Yuki. Her mother at university graduation. In this last photo, her mother wasn't yet thirty, her face softly lit and smiling up and out of the frame.

Decades younger, her mother might have looked less haggard, less tired, and less complicated by a lifetime of disappointments, but Hannah noticed none of this. The unspoken watchwords that best described Hannah's nature were that *the mind is its own place and in itself can make a heaven of hell, a hell of heaven,* and the beauty she saw in her mother's expression appeared unchanged by time. The photos were spread out all over the kitchen table when Hannah looked up and saw her mother grinning at them.

"Your father."

"Yes."

"Sentimental."

"You can't sleep?"

"Should have taken a pill maybe."

"Sit."

"There should be keepsakes in the wallet as well."

"There are. A movie ticket, an Air Canada boarding pass, and a petting zoo membership. Amazing."

"Your first movie, first plane ride, first time feeding a crab apple to a llama."

"Yes. I remember."

"I imagine your birth notice is in there too. Your first first."

"Your wedding announcement."

"Yes."

It was obvious why these items had meant much to her sentimental father. The story behind the laminated obituary, however, was not at all obvious. Hannah had never heard of Rosetta Johnson. Why was the announcement of her death and the short summary of her life in the wallet? Reading over the scant details of the deceased woman's lifetime, Hannah tried to make sense of it and could not. She did not worry, though. Her mother would explain.

Epilogue

Rosetta S. Johnson—Predeceased by Bernard "Bernie" Alexander Johnson, loving husband of 33 years and Pam, beloved sister. Cherished auntie to Gladys and Walter and great auntie to Sam, Tom, and Edwin. Services to be held October 12 at the McAllister Funeral at 9:00 and followed by interment at the Westgate Cemetery.

REVENGE PLOT WITH FISH

MacKendrick made the lunch reservation at Tierney from the hospital waiting room, and at the time, he hadn't known about the curved aquarium that stretched along the back wall of the restaurant. Standing at the hostess station and taking the place in, though, he thought the hundred-twenty gallon tank seemed an especially nice touch, a detail that would add an extra twist of bitterness to the scene of reprisal he'd imagined.

He requested a spot near the back and was led past tables that had mostly emptied out, the mid-week business lunch crowd come and gone. Quiet was good, he thought. As planned, his father wouldn't arrive for another half hour–more than enough time for MacKendrick to make a few pressing phone calls and still work out exactly what he wanted to say. What he wanted was alcohol, but with his father coming, he settled for coffee. MacKendrick hadn't slept in thirty some hours, so coffee was probably better anyway.

Inside the beautiful wood-finish aquarium were two dozen ugly fish circling around to nowhere. All one species, they were uneven black with orange flecks and had upturned mouths that gave them a look of arrogant pride. An aggressive species, MacKendrick figured, one that wouldn't live peaceably with others in a single tank. Maybe his server would know what they were.

All that he knew about tropical fish were the handful of names he remembered from early childhood. Malawi eyebiters, black phantom tetras, marbled hachetfish, bigspot barbs, and chocolate gouramis. Decades ago, tropical fish had been one of his father's asinine hobbies and enduring passions, a dinner topic he could hold court on at great length. Through repetition, the imaginative names had lodged in the memories of MacKendrick and his little brother Brian. The names stuck around much longer than their father.

The server returned with his coffee and a diminutive steel carafe of cream on a tray, and MacKendrick noticed that she was beautiful. Mid-twenties, her hazel hair worn up in a loose bun, held by some sort of clamp. When was it that the sight of such a lovely woman changed for MacKendrick? When was it that such soft clean skin and healthy beauty brought on more paternal thoughts than licentious ones? Heartened, he asked her about the fish.

"Oscars," she said.

"Oscars?"

MacKendrick was impressed.

"Oscar Cichlids."

With a blush, she admitted that customers asked all the time. "I don't really know anything about tropical fish."

Charming.

With a rush of affection, MacKendrick had the illogical urge to open his briefcase and show her the three fish he'd purchased from Pet Smart before coming to the restaurant. Such a gesture would have been odd, though, and he stopped himself. A lack of sleep made him distrust his own emotions, but he knew enough to keep his mouth closed.

"Oscar Cichlids." He gave a nod and explained he was waiting for someone.

"Call if you need anything."

The coffee was hot, but tired as he was, he drank down half the cup. The previous morning, shortly after he'd pulled into the MacKendrick Buick lot, Sylvia called to tell him she'd just spoken with the police. Brian had overdosed. His third overdose. That had been thirty-some hours ago, and MacKendrick had spent the night at St. Leonard in the ICU waiting room—trying not to dwell on the image of his little brother unconscious and unmoving in his hospital bed. The heart monitor. The IV line in and the catheter line out. The waiting room had a television, and MacKendrick flipped it on, dozing on and off in a hard-backed chair and dully staring at the History Channel. Elderly war criminals hiding in South America, Soviet gulags, and ethnic cleansings in God-knows-where for God-knows-what possible motive. The world could make you feel powerless, he thought. It wore away at you. At one point, MacKendrick fell into a half sleep and woke up again just as *From Russia with Love* was beginning. What business did James Bond have on the History Channel? MacKendrick didn't know, but he'd wound up watching the rest of the thing.

In Tierney, fortified from coffee, he took out his cell and telephoned the dealership. After Sylvia's call, he'd had to rearrange his schedule in a rush, but his floor manager was recently divorced and happy enough to come in on a day off. MacKendrick knew the business was doubtless under control, but two Regals were coming in that morning—one forest green and one river blue—and he wanted to make sure the odometers had been double checked before the receipts were signed. His second call was to the hospital, where he had to key through three separate automated menus before he was forwarded to the ICU. No changes from this morning. Brian still hadn't woken and his blood pressure was still down. MacKendrick thanked the unit nurse and called Sylvia.

"No change from last night," he said.

"Did you get his records sent over?"

"Not yet, but they know the history."

"Did you manage to get some sleep?"

"A few hours. Sort of"

"Come home."

"In a bit."

"Did you call your father?"

"I'm meeting him in a few minutes, actually."

"Meeting him?"

"Yeah, I'm in a restaurant waiting for him right now."

"In a restaurant?"

"Tierney."

"Tierney?"

"I haven't told him about the overdose yet."

"You didn't tell him Brian's in the hospital?"

MacKendrick fell silent. The questions were annoying him. He didn't have the energy to explain himself, and he wasn't sure he could have. But he had married well and Sylvia abandoned her questions. Okay, she said. The boys had gone off to school fine, and the house was quiet. She might pop out early for a few groceries before picking them up.

"What did you tell the boys last night?"

"Nothing. Said you had a business dinner. No point getting into it yet."

The thought of telling his sons about Brian flashed though MacKendrick's mind, making his throat tighten and face grow warm. He had to remind himself he was in public. He was in public, and he was emotional because he hadn't slept. Tearing up like an ass wouldn't help anyone. It was strange, he thought—and not for the first time—how very much alike paternal and fraternal affection could be. Maybe they occupied the same part of the brain. When the boys were young, he was forever calling one of them Brian by mistake. Being an older brother must have been good preparation for being a father. This had occurred to him before too. He hoped he would never let his boys down as he much as he had Brian.

"Still there?" Sylvia asked.

"Yes." His mind was jumping around, and he had to give his head a shake. "Just tired."

He needed to get off the phone, but promised to be home before dinner. He switched the cell to vibrate and caught sight of own reflection in the curved surface of the aquarium. The tank was probably some thick clear acrylic, custom made for the restaurant. Inside, green strands of cottony vine swayed, propelled by the submerged current of the water filter, he supposed. Two Oscar Cichlids drifted side by side and toward MacKendrick, through a decorative arched stone as if slowly promenading together. It was beautiful.

It was beautiful and very much unlike the images he recalled of his father's long-ago aquarium. Instead of dark, subtly sculpted stone, cheaply made figurines decorated the bottom of his father's fish tank. A sunken treasure chest containing rubies and jewels. A topless mermaid with painted cherry nipples wearing the most alluring of come-hither expressions. A miniature Poseidon wearing a seaweed crown and wielding a tiny trident. God, MacKendrick hadn't thought of that Poseidon in years. Though, maybe it was Neptune, now that he thought about it. Could the aquarium have been as tacky as he remembered, and how could his father have ever held the thing in such high value? And if it meant so very much, why would he keep it in the basement family room where young boys would be tempted to muck about with it?

Because their mother knew it was best that they not be underfoot when their father returned from work, MacKendrick and Brian spent much of their early childhood in that narrow townhouse basement. Save for an unfinished laundry-boiler area, the family room was the entire basement. Closed to company and full of secondhand furniture, it was where they went to avoid trouble and where they were sent when they were in trouble. Once they got in trouble for stuffing bananas in the Filtre Queen and switching the thing on just to see what would happen. Another time they got in trouble for peeing into the laundry room sink because the commercial breaks in between *Lucan, the Wolf Boy* weren't nearly long enough to run all the way up stairs and back down again. Another time, they melted an entire sixty-four colour box of crayolas on the driveway. Their father's punishments were predictably harsh but unpredictably creative. Scrub the driveway clean with toothbrushes. Write a hundred words explaining why their favourite television show was rubbish. Once, in a particularly inventive stroke, their father instructed them to select one toy from each other's shelves and destroy it. Was it a trick? If they cheated and chose something insignificant, would they get into more trouble? Too young to know, they betrayed one another as instructed. MacKendrick cut his brother's Stretch Armstrong open with a pair of scissors and Brian snapped off the wheels of MacKendrick's Evel Knievel supercycle.

The worst punishment was the aquarium. MacKendrick and Brian had eliminated the father's entire collection of tropical fish with a single healthy serving of Frosted Flakes scattered on the surface of the water. *They'rrrrre great!* Later, the brothers told each other that the cereal looked just like fish food flakes, but it was a lie they didn't believe. After scooping out the bodies and the mushy clumps of food, their father left the tank sitting in the basement family room and forbade anyone from cleaning it. The thing gave off a stale odour, but the smell was bad only up close. Worse was the sight of the thing. As the water evaporated, it left dusty brown rings around the inside of the glass. Weeks and months passed, and the water level slowly went down, down, down. Eventually, Poseidon and his trident poked up out of the surface of the water, and a few weeks after that, there was no water left at all. Just chalky synthetic pebbles that were once bright colours. The reminder was the punishment. The sight of the thing made MacKendrick feel powerless, but even at that young age, he recognized the cruelty as intentional, and in a way, the recognition lessened the punishment. Brian wasn't so lucky. His powerlessness wore away at him. The cell vibrated from within MacKendrick's jacket, and he checked the number before answering. It was Sylvia again.

"Why don't you just come home?"

"I'm all right."

"You can just tell your father about Brian over the phone, you know."

"I know."

They both went quiet. MacKendrick wondered who would break the silence first. He did.

"I'm all right," he repeated.

"The boys and I love you."

They said goodbye and MacKendrick slipped the cell back in his jacket. It'd been Sylvia's idea for him to reconnect with his father, and in some indefinable way, she must have felt sorry. At the time she'd been right, though. His father had left when he was ten and Brian seven–some twenty-five years had already passed, and as Sylvia said, the man couldn't possibly hurt MacKendrick anymore. The dealership was prospering and they had boys of their own. She was right of course. With his marriage and his children, his hatred had lost its full force. And though the old man had been a crap dad, he turned out to be a passable grandfather. He came to the boys' soccer games and remembered their birthdays. He hadn't had a drink in nearly twenty years, and that went a long way to changing his character.

The burmese border loach, the masked julie, the flowerhorn cichlid. MacKendrick found his mind was jumping around again. That morning, after leaving the hospital, he'd stopped in at a Pet Smart and walked slowly along the long walls of aquaria. Malawi eyebiters, black phantom tetras, marbled hachetfish, bigspot barbs, and chocolate gouramis, all the wonderful names were there. And then, at the end of an aisle, he found what he was looking for. The bettas, Siamese fighting fish. It was a scene in *From Russia with Love* that had given him the idea. In the movie, some evil mastermind described the east and west as Siamese fighting fish that will destroy one another, leaving them both vulnerable to SPECTRE. MacKendrick's idea was to buy three bettas, pour them into the same plastic baggie, and let the nasty little bastards sort it out amongst themselves. He would eat a nice lunch with his father and make sure he worked that long-ago aquarium into conversation. Then, at just the right moment, he would tell the old man about Brian's overdose and bring out the plastic baggie simultaneously. His father would get the message. Maybe the three fish would by then have all killed each other or maybe they'd still be fighting. Whichever. His father would get the message.

In the ICU, MacKendrick's tired mind had figured the revenge would be gratifying. Sitting in the restaurant and drinking his coffee now, though, he couldn't quite reassemble the logic of the thing. He was going to make his father feel guilt with a plastic baggie from Pet Smart? With dead or near-dead fish? Was that the thing of it? Bloody hell. It'd somehow made sense at four o'clock in the morning.

A bright sunlight came in as the front door at Tierney opened wide. MacKendrick squinted and saw his father at the hostess stand, steadying himself against it just the way MacKendrick had. The man looked impossibly old. Old and frail, like a war criminal hunted down in South America. MacKendrick understood that the baggie of dead or near-dead fish would stay in his briefcase. There was no point in taking them out. Even a sensible, well-executed revenge plot would make no difference. Instead, he would tell his father about the overdose, and they would feel sad and powerless together.

MASS GRAVES

Up until eight months, Mattie still took two naps a day, but at nine months, he doesn't seem to want even the one. Ten minutes in the rocking chair, his head will nod from time to time, but then it jolts right back up, and that's the end of that. Up against my shoulder while I pace, he will drift off after about twenty minutes, but if I put him down in the crib, he's awake and crying. The only way he wants to nap is the car—and I know—with gas at one thirty a litre and carbon dioxide emissions, circling Barrhaven for two hours a day is hardly responsible. After two or three blocks in the car, though, I check the rear view, and he's down. I wouldn't have tried this when we lived in Toronto or Montreal where drivers lean on the horn the second a red light turns green, but Ottawa drivers tend to be less aggressive. I think the Baby on Board sign helps too.

What do I do for the two-hour drive? My mind wanders mostly. I think about being a mother, and I think about my own mother and stepfather. Sometimes if I'm down, I think about my father, who was once estranged, but for a short time wasn't, and is now deceased. The roadside sign by the United Church is always good for an amusing typo. *Let Christ be your conscious. Except the lord into your life.* I've also noticed that a good number of the street names in our neighbourhood are no more than compounds of geographic nouns. We have a *Glenmeadow,* a *Meadowfield,* and a *Fieldbriar.* Toward the library, the emphasis is less on flora and more on fauna: *Deerfox, Foxhound,* and *Houndboar.* Today, I'm circling around an enclave of new townhomes and two-bedroom singles, and I notice a sign that reads *Mass Graves.*

On second glance, it's actually *Moss Groves,* which is a far more reasonable street name. The mistake makes me think, though; I've had these momentary misreadings for as long as I can remember. If I'm reading on the bus, for example, and not really paying attention, letter combinations somehow rearrange themselves. *Infant* can become *instant* or *dressing gown* can become *dressing down*. A couple of years ago, when we still lived in Toronto, I was walking down Yonge and out of the corner of my eye, I misread a movie marquee for *Original Sin* as *Origami Sin*. *Origami Sin* with Antonio Banderas—yes, I'd pay to see that.

As my mind wanders more, it occurs to me that maybe these mental lapses are like inner Freudian slips—mistakes that can inadvertently reveal one's mental state. It makes sense. If outgoing slips of the tongue are meaningful, then why wouldn't incoming tricks of the eye?

"Anderson is looking after the provincial grants this year."

"Is that a promotion for him?" I ask.

Peter doesn't answer, but I can feel him shrugging next to me in bed.

"I was hoping for the assignment," he says.

It's only nine but we're in bed already, chatting in the dark before sleep. Peter lets me go on about how Mattie turned the dial on his chatterbox telephone for the first time, I let him go on about work, and then we'll fall asleep exhausted. This is how things are now.

"Did you hear that?"

"What?"

I can feel him shrugging again.

"Did I check the basement door?" he asks.

"You did."

Ever since Mattie, Peter has been a bit compulsive. Is the basement door locked? Because home invaders could come in and that'd be it. Is the door to the garage pulled shut? Because carbon dioxide could drift upstairs and that'd be it. Is the iron unplugged and back in the cupboard? Because Mattie could pull on the cord and that'd be it.

"I walked with Adams at lunch today," he says. "Only thirty minutes but we went at a good clip and the exercise felt good."

Peter works in an office for a non-profit, where they collect subsidies from various revenue streams and disperse funds to emerging visual artists in the capital region. It's not exactly glamorous, but as Peter points out, with two Fine Arts degrees, any job with a salary and family benefits will do. Up until Mattie, it also gave him leisure time for the gym or indoor soccer.

"Do you ever misread words?"

I tell him about driving Mattie for his nap and what occurred to me that afternoon.

"So *Mass Graves* means what?" he asks.

"I don't know."

Since he doesn't seem all that interested, I don't pursue the topic, and after a few minutes of quiet, I guess we've agreed it is time to sleep. I can't seem to shake the thought, though. If *Mass Graves* does mean something–if the misreading does reflect something about my mental state–well, it can't be anything good.

Once, during a three-hour layover in Winnipeg, I read this magazine article about the top five causes of stress. Death of a child, death of a spouse, divorce, job loss, and new job. Divorce might have come before death of a spouse–which makes more sense, really. Nonetheless, if this magazine was right and causes of stress can be quantified and enumerated so neatly, then maternity leave should really be on that list somewhere. In a way, it's the end of one job and the start of another. So maybe I am depressed. I don't necessarily miss my accounting position with the city, but I was upset when I learned my cubicle had been reassigned.

"I swear I can hear something scratching," Peter says.

Then I hear it too. The sound isn't really a scratching, though; it's more like something scurrying overhead.

In the morning, Mattie is in the highchair and I'm listening to *Ottawa This Week* on the kitchen radio–I like to keep up with community events I won't be attending–when Peter calls in from the front door. I can't make out what he's saying, and I'm a little annoyed that he's dragged me all the way over from the kitchen.

"I think I found our problem." He points through the narrow window in the hall and gestures for me to come closer.

"I'm feeding him the pabulum," I say. "You couldn't just come in and tell me?"

"I already have my shoes on." Peter shrugs and apologizes, but I can tell he isn't really sorry.

Outside, a chipmunk streaks from the side fence and cuts across to the steps. It runs impossibly fast and disappears.

"They're going under the steps," Peter says.

"They?"

"Yeah, this is the third or fourth one I've seen."

Our front step is no more than a long concrete slab with this fake wood rail that came with the house.

"Our step is hollow?"

He shrugs.

"I've got to get back to Mattie."

"All right." Peter checks his watch. "I'm not going to get a seat on the bus." He's nodding to himself but hasn't made any move to leave. "Is he eating the pabulum?"

"Just spits it out."

"The book says to keep trying."

It's October, and the wind is cold today, so Mattie and I stay only ten minutes at the playground. Afterwards, I park the stroller at the front of the house and take a closer look at the steps. I can't really see where a chipmunk might get in, but the ground beside the patio stones is disturbed. Brown dirt has been kicked outward by the looks of it, and once I tilt up a few of the stones, I see that the chipmunks have dug a whole network of furrows. It looks kind of neat. The path weaves left and then right and at one point, it forks. Seen from above, the whole thing looks like one of those bisections of ant hills they have at the Nature Museum.

Ingenious. It's admirable in a way.

"So how do you think they get from the front step to the attic?"

Peter's mouth is full, and for whatever reason, he waits until he's swallowed before responding with a shrug.

"I can't imagine there's anything up there," I say. "Foam insulation and exposed beams."

Our walk-in closet has an access door to the attic in the ceiling, but we've never been up there. Like most of Barrhaven, the developers threw up our entire neighbourhood in no time flat. The one time we tried the attic door, we found it painted shut.

"In between the walls?" I ask.

In his highchair, Mattie has knocked his sippy cup on its side, watery apple juice dripping onto the plastic tray until Peter turns it right-side up.

"Do you think they sneak up between the walls?" I repeat.

He shrugs.

"What I imagine is like a prison movie," I say. "The chipmunks are making a break and they go through cinder block and then squeeze in between the dry wall, inching along bit by bit. Once in a while, they might hit upon a metal pipe that they can't get through, so they all have to double back and find a new route. One chipmunk would be the wizened old con and then another one could be the brash young upstart who just started doing his time."

Peter nods. "Yeah, I can see that."

That Saturday, after picking up a few groceries, Peter stops off at the Canadian Tire and comes home with a five-pound bag of blood meal.

"The guy in the garden centre said it should do the trick."

Blood meal. When we slice open the bag in the garage, I half-expect the soil will be a vivid scarlet in colour, but it just looks like normal dirt. Maybe a bit darker than the top soil we put in the box garden last year, but nothing too memorable. To spread the stuff around, we lift up the patio stones again, and it's a pain.

With the side of his sneaker, Peter brushes around the exposed earth, collapsing and filling in the chipmunks' elaborate system of furrows in less than a minute. All that industriousness, gone in a few kicks.

"We just have to sprinkle the blood meal," he says. "The guy said we might also try hair in a stocking."

"Hair in a stocking?"

"Yeah. Clean out one or two of your hairbrushes and put the hair in old nylons or panty hose."

"Really? Was this some fifteen-year-old kid working in the garden centre by any chance?"

Peter doesn't even look up to respond. "It wasn't some kid. And the guy seemed to know what he was talking about. It's the scent that keeps the chipmunks away."

I want to say the idea sounds like witchcraft to me. The blackest of the black arts. If human hair and used panty hose don't work, will we move onto toenail clipping or menstrual blood? Peter doesn't seem like he's in the mood, though.

"Is the monitor turned all the way up?" he asks.

Mattie is in his playpen in the living room, the Fisher Price monitor standing guard, but Peter doesn't always trust the thing.

"It is."

While we're trying to put them back in place, one of the patio stones slips and hits the side of the front step, cracking the square stone from one corner to the other. The break is an almost perfect diagonal and the two triangles pieces are nearly symmetrical. The odds against such an accident have got to be astronomical, but Peter is concerned only with where we're going to find a replacement.

It rains that night and for the next two days, washing away the blood meal and diluting any horrifying scent that might have been on my panty hose. The guy at the Canadian Tire suggests cement paper and cashew butter. The store doesn't carry them, but in a conspiratorial voice, he tells us we can find them in the Rona three blocks down.

In the car, I admit to Peter that the guy did sound like he knew what he was talking about.

"Quite knowledgeable about rodents," I say.

"Didn't I say?"

"Cashew butter sounds delicious."

At home, we drop dollops of the stuff in the middle of a half dozen sheets of cement paper. As we spoon it out, it smells great and I am tempted, but the jar strictly warns against human consumption. When we're all done, we stand inside the front hall and consider our work through the window. It looks absurd, as if we've dropped papers all over our lawn and just left them there.

"I guess it's the same principle as fly paper," I say. "But horizontal."

"As long as it works."

"And what do we do with all the chipmunks frozen in their tracks?"

Peter shrugs beside me and lets out an amused exhale. "I hadn't thought that far ahead."

By the next evening, all the cashew butter is gone, but we don't find any chipmunks frozen in their tracks. On one of the sheets of cement paper, there is a leftover fragment of tail. *Look at that fine piece of tail,* I think but don't say. The thing just looks like a tuft of coarse fur at first, but when I pick up the cement paper, I can see it's definitely a part of the animal's appendage, ripped off with a bit of dried blood left over. It's horrifying.

I'm still thinking about the sight of the tail fragment hours later, but it doesn't seem like something I might reasonably start an argument over, so we fight over the thermostat instead. Peter doesn't think we should turn the furnace on before November and I think we should turn it on whenever we feel cold—as far as arguments go, it's a reliable standby, and it can escalate pretty fast.

I feed Mattie his dinner in the kitchen, and Peter eats in the front of the computer upstairs.

"What's the worst that could happen?"

The scurrying above our bedroom occurs more often at night, and we hear it only every few days, but it has gotten louder. The original few chipmunks seem to have invited over their entire extended family.

"The worst?"

Peter shrugs beside me in bed and lets his voice trail off. We're in a post coital cuddling mode, and he's more inclined to sidestep any kind of conflict.

"They could set up home up there," Peter says after a moment. His tone of voice sounds defeated. "They could nest up there, store food all over the place, reproduce, gnaw away at the support beams and electrical wiring, leave droppings all over the place."

"Grow old and die peacefully," I add.

We're quiet a moment more and then he tells me that we do have to get rid of them. Which, of course, I know. It's just that the torn-off bit of tail freaked me out a bit.

"The sight of it, that's all."

They're rodents, I know, and it's not as if I'm vegetarian or ever objected to a pair of leather heels. Fur, I don't care for, but who does? Really, I don't know what my problem is.

The next day, we drive over to the Home Depot and purchase a medium-size pest trap-and-release cage, which comes close to seventy dollars with the tax. To justify the expense, I point out the ingenuity of the cage: the wire box is rectangular with entrances at both ends. The one-way doors silently lock into place after the animals have entered and they aren't even aware that they're trapped.

"Think of the teams of mechanical engineers and all the effort that went into designing this thing," I say.

The cage does get results. When we go to the front hall the next morning, three chipmunks are inside the cage. I would have thought they'd be frantic to find themselves captives, but they're all just standing there, as if loitering.

"Can you take care of this?" Peter asks as he checks his watch.

He really hates not getting a seat on the bus.

"Sure."

The guy at the store said the chipmunks would have to be released at least fifteen kilometres away from where they were captured, so when it's naptime, I head south to Manotick, a village just outside of Barrhaven. Before Mattie was born, Peter and I came here a few times–once for a pumpkin carving contest and once for a used book sale at the library—and he always made a fuss about the small town charm. He said *smalltowncharm* as if it were one word, and I teased him about it.

Near the bridge, I pull onto the gravel shoulder and remove the caged chipmunks from the trunk. Setting the cage down, I feel a bit like a kidnapper kicking hostages out the side of a van and peeling away.

"Be good." I wave farewell.

Mattie is still asleep in the back, so I drive around to stretch out his nap. The roadside sign by the United Church says *3nails+1Christ=4giveness,* and I can't help it, but the stupidity of the thing cheers me right up.

Over the next week, I'm back in Manotick setting free chipmunks on four separate occasions, but I choose different drop-off spots: a couple of public parks, the side of a rural road, and once next to the library. Some thirteen chipmunks if my count is right. I wonder if I'm disrupting the local ecosystem in some way. Nonetheless, the cage isn't working. The scurrying sounds overhead aren't going away. The little critters are either navigating their way back home to our attic or we have an inexhaustible supply of chipmunks.

Today, I not only finagle pabulum and apple purée into Mattie, I also manage to put him down in his crib for naptime. Mother of the year, that's me. Then, as I'm coming downstairs, I happen to look up at just the right second and spot someone through the front hall window—someone who is lifting his arm and about to ring the doorbell and undo my hard-won victory. I must look like a madwoman from the attic because I swear I hurdle the banister, fling myself through the foyer, and pull open the front door in a matter of half a second.

"I just put the baby down." I'm breathless. "Please don't ring the bell."

The two boys at the door look up at me in unison.

"Good afternoon, Miss."

The Church of Latter Day Saints. Seventh Day Adventists. Jehovah's Witnesses. Mormons. I can't tell the difference. Is there a difference? They can't be anymore than seventeen or eighteen years old. Healthy-looking young men in grey ties with short-sleeve dress shirts, white and carefully pressed in that proselytizer way.

"Do you mind if we ask you about your afterlife?"

"Oh. Certainly. Not at all."

I have to remind myself to be kind. After all, these people are trying to save me, and given all the harm that people can do to one another, there are certainly worse motivations.

"Do you belong to a particular church?"

"I'm afraid not."

The one closest to me seems to be doing all the talking. The other kid is just standing there grinning—the serene, beatific smile of the saved. Hiding behind the screen door feels wrong, so I step outside to listen and nod.

"Were you raised with religion?"

"Not particularly."

My estranged father was a Baptist who didn't much care about faith until cancer spread throughout both his lungs. I was raised by an Anglican mother who didn't practice and a Jewish stepfather who didn't observe. We had a Christmas tree, but it didn't have an angel or a star on top or anything. All of this seems like too much to explain at my front door.

"Well, my name is Timothy, and my friend Isaac and I are in your neighbourhood today to talk about the Church of Latter Day

Saints and the joy that we have found in giving our lives over to our Lord and Saviour."

Well, my name is Helen and now I suppose I'm more-or-less obliged to listen to the end of the spiel. Sometimes, I think hell isn't other people, but the ability to see other people's points of view. Stupid empathy.

What amazes me is just how sure of themselves these young men are. What gives a seventeen-or-eighteen-year-old such certainty? What makes them think they know the first thing about anything? How can these two young men stand there and presume to give advice to a woman twenty years older than they are? I listen for two or three minutes more and then the silent kid finally speaks.

"Don't you want your baby to find heaven?"

That night, Peter greets me through Mattie.

"Hello, big boy. And how was your day with Mommy?"

"Tell Daddy how well you slept."

"Daddy had a long conference call to Toronto this morning."

Without ever agreeing to, we sometimes communicate through Mattie. I suppose all parents of infants do.

"Ask Daddy how the call went."

"Went too long. No time for a walk at lunch."

We'll have to stop these proxy conversations at some point. I mean, if we're still talking through our son when he's thirteen or eighteen or whatever, we'll really screw him up.

"Tell Mommy that the chipmunks will leave on their own if there is a cat or a dog in the house."

"Really?"

"Daddy read it on the internet. And it's not like the dog or cat has to be a hunter. It's just a threat that will scare away the chipmunks."

The idea sounds like a good one, and we scrutinize it through-out dinner and most of the evening. Cats and dogs can be good companions for a little kid. They can help teach affection and responsibility. Peter and I both had cats growing up, so we're lean-ing towards a cat. A cat is more independent. And neither of us really has the energy to walk a dog. Female cats are less territorial. Would she be an indoor cat or an outdoor cat? In bed, we're trying to settle on the right cat name, and the conversation turns.

"Has Mattie been tested for allergies yet?" Peter asks.

"There's no cat allergy on my side of the family."

"Can't these things be recessive for a few generations?"

"Cat feces are toxic to pregnant women. Does that mean it's toxic to babies?"

He shrugs beside me. Our conversation slows down, punctuated with long pauses.

"Cats shed all over the place."

"Mattie still puts his hand in his mouth all the time."

"I don't agree with de-clawing a cat."

"Neither do I."

We give the cage another few days until I admit it isn't really work-ing. All three exterminators I contact say there is no way to get rid of chipmunks without killing them. The last guy is the rudest.

"That's kind of what *exterminator* means."

Fumigation is apparently the best method, and we'd have to stay in a hotel for a week, which is pretty much impossible with Mattie. There might still be lingering odours after a week too, and it isn't worth taking the chance.

I'm already in a bad mood when Peter comes home with another idea from the internet.

"A bucket filled with water and sunflower seeds."

I don't understand at first.

"You fill the bucket with water and then cover the surface with sunflower seeds. The chipmunk leans over to get a seed and falls in."

"It drowns?"

"It drowns."

"How many chipmunks can you drown?"

"You don't have to. A few die and the others see the bodies and—"

"And word gets around?"

"I suppose."

We're silent through dinner. After Mattie goes to sleep, I watch television downstairs and he watches a show on the office computer. He feels one way and I feel another, so there's not much room for reasonable debate.

In bed, we try anyway. I say we might give the cage more time. He says it's been over a week. I say we could buy a large cage or a second medium-sized one. He says the cages cost too much. It's an unproductive but civilized argument, and then, Peter breaks the rules of engagement.

"What if one of these things hurts Mattie? Don't you care?"

Against my wishes, he drives to Costco the next day and returns with two twenty-litre buckets and five pounds of sunflower seeds. They're salted, and I can't help thinking about the chipmunks' blood pressure.

The buckets don't seem to be working for the first few days, but their presence on our front lawn has meant Peter's been sleeping in the upstairs office for the whole time. I don't want the buckets to work, of course, and I don't even really want to look at them. Every day, as I carry Mattie out to the car for our naptime drive, though, there they are, and I can't stop myself from taking a quick glance to see if the surface of seeds has been disrupted.

All is fine until the fourth day, when I chance a closer look. Sunflower seeds still cover the top of the water, but when I knock the bucket with my toe, they part in spots, revealing three chipmunks drifting at the bottom. The water method has been working all along. I start to cry as I buckle Mattie into his car seat with Mr. Snuggles, and there something about crying in front of my child that makes me want to cry more. We take *Bisonwolf* all the way down to *Elkheron* and as always, circling the neighbourhood soothes Mattie to sleep, and I calm down too. What I can't do, though, is put the chipmunks from my mind; it was stupid of me not to expect the sight of them, but the sudden appearance of their froze-up little bodies did shock me. They had that taxidermy combination of being very lifelike and very much dead all at once. Of the many painful ways to die, drowning has to be up high on that list.

The afternoon I was brought into obstetrics, one of the nurses kept asking me to measure my pain on a scale of one to ten, and I remember it baffled me at the time. I wanted to ask if pain could be quantified and if so, how—but such a response would have been ridiculously out of place. I think I wound up saying six. What would drowning rate? Close to ten, I imagine.

Near the end, my father's lungs were so bad that he had trouble breathing. He said he knew the air was there and that he should logically be able to pull it into his lungs, but something inexplicable simply didn't work. His first reaction was panic and if one of his oxygen tanks was beside him, he'd reach for it desperately. After a few seconds without air, he said his mind clouded to fanciful delusions pretty quickly. This is what drowning must be.

I'm stopped at a red light and I'm crying again. I close my eyes and lean my head against the steering wheel. It feels like no more than a second, but it must be more because I hear a blaring horn. I open my eyes and see that the traffic lights have turned green.

The blaring horn is the car behind me honking. With such noise, Mattie wakes and his wails fill the car instantly.

I turn to glare out the back window. The driver is a kid in his mid-twenties, driving some sporty Honda model in red. We make eye contact and the kid's hands flip upward from the steering wheel in disgust. I turn to face forward, put the car into park and switch on the hazard lights.

OH, THE PLACES YOU'LL GO!

Virginia Bishop was a middle child, and though she wouldn't have accepted the psychology of such an explanation, she grew up with a middle child's troubles. On the one day a week her father wasn't off managing Bishop's South Hasting Chevrolet, he could be found in the Belleville Hockey Arena bellowing his encouragement for Virginia's older brother. And while Virginia's mother did not work outside of the house, her approach to the management and administration of the Bishop household was no less conscientious and rigorous than her husband's at the dealership, and so young Virginia was often left to her own devices. Her earliest memories were set inside a playpen, where she sat turning the pages of library picture books while her mother vacuumed and shampooed the upstairs or balanced the family chequebooks at the dining room table. Virginia would have been four years old at the time, certainly old enough to climb free from the confinement of a playpen, but even at that age, she somehow knew her need for attention could not contend with her mother's single-mindedness. It was not until the birth of a third child and the subsequent tubal ligation that her mother revealed any obvious maternal feelings, and few of them were directed at Virginia.

Thus, Virginia grew inward throughout her formative years and emerged into adolescence a defiantly independent and wholly conflicted teen: self-contained and confident enough to attract the boys in Hasting Junior High and Quinte Secondary School, but also needy and isolated enough to allow their advances. As a freshman and sophomore, she dated the junior boys with driver's licenses—Julian Henry, Walter Craig, William Daniel—and as a junior and senior, she tended toward young university men with cars of their own–Andrew Nelson, Robert Malcolm, Simon Trevor. Much of the appeal was getting out of Belleville, which she found far too limited. Her gentlemen callers took her to Tweed to pick blueberries or to Picton to make out on the Sandbanks. Because the demands of the Ontario secondary school were less than demanding for Virginia–diagramming sentences, provincial capitals, and photosynthesis–the opportunity to leave Belleville behind her came in the form of a scholarship to the University of Toronto, where she later dated yet another older man: Christopher Todd, the graduate teaching assistant who ran her lab in second-year psychology class PSY2078 Family Dynamics and the father of her unexpected son.

Duncan Todd's first memory was set in a redbrick townhouse in North York–he and his mother seated together on the chesterfield reading *Oh, the Places You'll Go!*–but the family actually lived in graduate student housing for over a year prior to the townhouse. Because he was no more than an infant at the time, Duncan had no actual memory of the dormitory, but his mother had later reminisced about his infancy so much that he sometimes felt he could put together a pretty good account of that period.

Resting in his bassinet but awake, infant Duncan sat propped up against a blanket while his mother reviewed her class notes. She looked tired because she was tired. Her third semester of university had also been her second trimester of pregnancy, and it had been no picnic sitting Christmas exams with a round belly and an inflatable doughnut under her butt. She and Christopher Todd had legally married–for their son and for the OSAP money handed out to married students with dependents–but her husband hadn't turned out to be all that she'd hoped. He'd managed to put together a thesis proposal in Psychology–something to do with the connection between learned helplessness and violent impulses–but the guy was dragging his feet and hadn't yet tackled the hard work of drafting, revising, and editing. Meanwhile, Virginia was left with the task of fulltime student and fulltime mother.

From his vantage point in the bassinet, the infant Duncan understood none of these troubles, of course. All he understood was that the woman who was his mother looked unhappy, crying and yelling and knocking the textbooks in her lap onto the floor.

"No, no, no, no," she said.

It was there and then, she later explained, that she knew she would never have a second child. At the same moment, she decided that school and motherhood simply did not work together, and she decided she'd had enough of Christopher Todd's dragging feet. He could switch from the thesis stream to the coursework stream, take an additional class and an independent study over the summer and have his Master's degree by September. That should be enough for a halfway decent job by the fall.

Duncan watched his mother crying a bit more, and then she stopped. Lifting him out of the bassinet, she hugged him close.

"I won't leave you sitting alone in a playpen," she said.

The halfway decent job her reluctant husband found was an administrative position at a municipal mental health centre, but–Virginia told herself–it was an entry-level job with room for growth and it paid well enough for her to spend her days home with Duncan in their North York townhouse. She sometimes thought about her unfinished degree, but mostly, she was happy to pass her time pushing the stroller to the library or watching her son play with the other children in the park.

By the time Duncan was in senior kindergarten, she could see what a wonderfully sensitive young boy he'd become. If the children in the playground varied in age from toddler to preteen, Duncan suggested

Red Light, Green Light or Red Rover, games that could include everyone, and if there were only rough and tumble boys around, Duncan would adapt, falling into War, Tag, or Grounders just as easily. Her son befriended the mildest of children, and his best friend was a runty little boy named Byron who had an unfortunate harelip. Virginia's favourite playground memory occurred when Duncan stepped in to settle a Tag dispute by turning the target on himself.

"I'm it," he yelled.

New to the Mental Health Centre of Vaughan, Christopher Todd missed much during these formative years, and so in bed at night, Virginia tried to convey the highlights of their son's days as best she could. Tired and frustrated from work, her husband most often rolled away, his indifference all too apparent, and on days when he was especially irritable, he would question the way she was raising Duncan, accusing her of spoiling and coddling their son. He once even suggested that such maternal attention might not be good for the boy, and while he did not use the term *mama's boy* outright, Virginia suspected that was what he was thinking. It was a disappointing oversimplification from a supposedly educated man, and Virginia told him so.

This attitude alone might not have been cause to end the marriage, but by the time Duncan began junior high, Virginia had returned to university, earning the last of her remaining degree credits while her disappointment of a husband was still slogging away in the same entry-level administrative position. It wasn't easy to admit that these failures were due to a lack of ambition, and it wasn't easy to decide that Duncan was better off without such a male role model, but these are the conclusions Virginia eventually reached.

Duncan did not have happy memories of junior high. On top of his father's departure and his mother's new boyfriend, Duncan was on the chubbier side as a preteen—just five or so extra pounds that his mother assured him would be gone soon enough—but adolescence can be unkind even to those without additional weight. His mother swore that once he shed the last of the baby fat, he'd be left with fine cheek bones and a strong jaw that girls would covet. The other reason junior high was less than pleasant—though Duncan would never admit to this reason, not even to himself—was his friendship with Byron. Adolescence can be extremely unkind to those with a harelip. The sight of his friend being teased or picked on brought about a surge of loyalty in Duncan, a sudden and violent flood of self-righteousness that twice wound up in someone getting punched. Left to themselves after that, Duncan and Byron spent much of their time together, cultivating the fanatical obsessions with movies and music that can consume best friends before girls. Years later, what Duncan remembered most was how they laughed and laughed. What were they laughing at all the time?

Virginia understood why her son and his odd friend laughed at Hiram Alexander as much as they did. Seven years her senior, Hiram was short and wore an unflattering pair of wire-rimmed spectacles that made him appear even older, and in the eyes of a young boy, real estate law would not be the most glamorous of professions. What her son did not know was how this quiet, timid man put her mind at rest. She worried a great deal and what she often worried about was her son. His weight problem, his insular friendship with runty little Byron. PSY4056 Group Processes in Social Psychology had taught her these developments could stunt his maturation and ambition. Hiram provided reassurance.

"Duncan will come into his own, on his own."

Talking in bed with Hiram was much more soothing than it had been with Christopher Todd. All young boys have their obsessions, Hiram assured her. Normal and expected for adolescents the world around. When she asked him if he'd been that way, Hiram didn't answer, but she felt him shrug beside her in bed. It was this moment that convinced her that her dependable suitor would make a dependable role model and stepfather.

At first, the dramatic arts class was no more to Duncan than a required credit–less painful than choral music or painting. Once on the theatre stage at Vaughan Collegiate, however, he felt immediately at ease. For whatever reason, he didn't possess any of his classmates' anxiety or self-consciousness, and once he figured out how to project his voice throughout the small school theatre, there wasn't much to acting. In February, posters for the spring play started appearing in the hallway. It was *Of Mice and Men,* and after reading through a library copy, Duncan thought he'd audition to be one of the farmhands. His mother, though, said he should be more ambitious.

"There's no reason you couldn't get a lead role."

She would run lines with him, she said. Help him with all that memorization. Although the leads usually went to seniors, Duncan ended up auditioning for and playing George. As he'd thought, the memorization was difficult, but character traits and emotions were easy enough to fake, and all in all, acting wasn't nearly as difficult as trigonometry, political science and essay composition, subjects for which he needed and accepted Byron's help.

The school play positioned Duncan well at Vaughan Collegiate, placing him near the upper middle of the high school hierarchy and introducing him to the world of girls. As his mother had once predicted, he outgrew his baby fat and was left with fine cheek bones and a strong jaw. First there was Cheryl Kate, the senior who was playing Curley's wife. She put her tongue in his mouth after dress rehearsal. Then, there was Donna Helen, the lighting director who thrust his hand under her shirt during the cast party. Then, Janet Rosemary–took off her blouse and camisole in a stairwell during the freshman semiformal. Sarah Madison–her hand in his pants behind the special education portables. Rachel Lillian–showed up in the cafeteria in a skirt with no underwear. And all before the end of grade ten. None of them, however, let Duncan go as far as Madeline Nichol.

Virginia loved seeing her sensitive son on stage. After playing George so convincingly in *Of Mice and Men,* Duncan went on to Peter in *A Zoo Story,* Happy in *Death of a Salesman,* and Torvald in *A Doll's House* over the next few semesters. While she believed he could play any part well, her son excelled not in flashy characters, but in roles that were deliberately restrained–the men who were everyman, men with great stores of quiet integrity. And it was no coincidence, of course; his greatest qualities as an actor were also his greatest qualities as a sensitive young man. Virginia thoroughly enjoyed each of her son's performances, and more than that, memorizing lines together gave her an excuse to spend time with her son, who, as he grew older, needed her less and less.

Because her son needed her less and because her Psychology degree remained unused in any practical manner, Virginia decided on graduate school. Work wasn't necessary. The mortgage was paid off and Hiram's income more than covered living expenses. She did make sure she was around the house in the evening, though. She'd studied PSY4333 Human Sexuality and knew better than to leave a nearly-seventeen-year-old boy alone with his hormones and a girl. Madeline Nichol was a particular cause for concern. The young woman seemed no more adept at trigonometry, political science, or essay composition than Duncan, and yet she showed up at their door every other day to tutor him. She also had the use of her family Volvo station wagon, a sign of questionable parenting if ever there was one. Once, passing by the den to eavesdrop, Virginia overheard the two of them running lines together and she found it hard not to dislike the girl even further.

The play was *The Medea,* and though he'd gotten the role of Jason, Duncan was having trouble understanding the story. She kills her own children to get back at her husband? Would a mother do that?

"Why don't we just read the lines a few more times?" Madeline asked.

She leaned over and patted his knee. They were on the den chesterfield, and concentrating with her so close by was hard, especially when she slipped her shoes off at the heel and tucked her feet up under herself. Duncan's better judgement told him that his mother was still somewhere in the house, but he eventually broke down, and playful cuddling led to heavy petting.

"Why don't we go out for a drive?" she asked.

With the station wagon, they could have climbed into the back, but Madeline preferred to have sex in the passenger seat with the back rest all the way down. For nearly six months, they parked behind the community recreation centre once or twice a week, and Duncan got so used to this ritual that he was shocked and entirely lost the first time she broke up with him. For Christ sake, they'd talked about living together for university and marrying afterward. They'd exchanged Valentine's presents, birthday presents, and Christmas presents, and he couldn't understand that they might not always be together. For Christmas, she'd even given him a pewter tree ornament, engraved with their names on one side and *Our First Noel* on the other.

The first time her son and that girl broke up, Duncan sought Virginia out in the dining room. Up late finishing work on a paper for her PSY5033 Psychopathologies of Adolescence seminar, she tried to be understanding while listening to her son's romantic troubles. Befuddled as he was, Duncan kept on repeating that he didn't understand what had happened. He was stifling tears that clearly embarrassed him.

"You don't have to be at all ashamed of your sensitivity," she told him.

He started on about some Christmas tree ornament she'd given him, and how he'd thought that the engraving meant that they'd have many many holidays together. What Virginia felt, of course, was relief–better to be done with Madeline Nichol and her station wagon–but she didn't let these thoughts show on her face. Virginia acted as sympathetic as she could and did not let herself smile until she related the news to Hiram the next morning.

"Poor guy," Hiram said.

He suggested they do something nice to cheer Duncan up. Maybe a big gesture. The basement needed renovating, he said, and they might consider giving Duncan a bit more privacy: there was certainly space for a new bedroom and bath downstairs. Eighteen years old in the spring, Duncan would be deciding on a university soon, and the renovation might just give him reason to stay closer to home. A separate entrance would cost some, but they could call it part of his birthday present.

After the contractors were all finished, Virginia did the decorating herself, selecting a flecked beige berber for the carpeting and a medium tan paint for the large room and walk-in closet. She picked out a few framed prints and spent a little too much on a full length mirror that caught her eye. It was a good three feet wide, six feet tall, and framed by a subtle hand-carved border. Pricey, but a touch she was proud of.

The new basement was completed in February, a few weeks before Duncan's eighteenth birthday. Unbeknownst to Virginia, her son and Madeline Nichol had by then gotten back together, broken up, and gotten back together again. That Duncan did not seek her out and confide in her on any of these occasions did, of course, hurt.

§

The first time, they were apart for eight days, and then, Madeline called him in tears. The trouble had all been a misunderstanding, she claimed; something a friend of someone in one of her classes said he'd heard about Duncan, and she'd broken it off with him all too impulsively. What could Duncan say in response? Her impulsiveness was part of her passion, and her passion was part of what appealed to him, and so they got back together. Then there was another misunderstanding, another impulsive break-up, and another passionate reunion. It was a cycle that repeated a number of times.

"I don't get it," Byron told him. "Set some ground rules. Why let her walk all over you?"

The reason was sex, but Duncan wasn't about to admit this to himself. With a separate entrance and unlimited privacy, he was sleeping with Madeline three, four, and five times a week. A basement apartment beat the heck out of a station wagon. On his eighteenth birthday, they'd tried oral sex together, and it was a feeling that convinced Duncan they would never be apart again.

That was not the case, though, and when they broke up the week before senior prom, Madeline confessed she'd been sleeping with a friend of someone in one of her classes for over a month.

All young men have their romantic dramas, Hiram assured her. Normal for eighteen-year-olds the world around. Virginia knew he was right, and she was best to distance herself from the trouble, but as she sat at the dining room table finalizing the wording of a thesis proposal she'd entitled *Self Image and Personality Development,* the sound of Duncan's sobs came up from the basement. He was sitting on the floor beside his bed when she opened the door, and this time, he wasn't at all embarrassed by his tears. In fact, he was sobbing so much that his hunched-over body shook, gasping loudly with each inhale. What had happened to her confident son? What had happened to the self-contained young man who played everyman characters with dignity and restraint? Rubbing his back, she calmed her son and coaxed him to sit up on the bed, listening silently while he once again belaboured the details of his past with Madeline Nichol. It was another hour until he exhausted himself with explaining and then he told her what hurt most.

"I feel just helpless, you know?"

Virginia wanted to leave.

After telling his mother all that could, Duncan felt better, but he was surprised when she patted his back one more time and stood to leave.

"Hiram will be home shortly," she said.

Duncan wasn't sure if this meant he should talk to Hiram later or if they'd all go out to dinner together or what. Her mood was hard to read. And then, her voice trailed off and she was gone.

"I'll come up in a little while," he said after her, but it was just something to say.

Strangely, Duncan felt disconnected from his earlier distress and the events of the day, as if they were a distant memory or someone else's problems altogether. The top of his desk was a mess, he noticed, and he stood to straighten it, aligning the spines of his library books into a neat stack. They made him think of his mother, who had taken him to the public library for as long as he could remember. She said reading built sensitivity and ambition.

In fact, his first memory was of them sitting on the chesterfield reading a library book in the redbrick townhouse in North York.

Oh, the Places You'll Go. She dropped the ends of sentences and encouraged him to finish each one.

"*With banner flip-flapping, once more you'll ride—*"

"High."

"*Ready for anything under the—*"

"Sky."

"*Ready because you're that kind of—*"

"Guy!"

Duncan caught his self image in the elaborate full-length mirror his mother had bought for his bedroom, and he lashed out. He hit the glass, sending a crack outward, and it felt so good that he hit it again. The last time he'd punched anyone or anything was defending Byron in junior high, and Duncan had forgotten what a welcome release violence could be. He was still punching at the mirrored glass when his friend telephoned and said he'd heard about Madeline.

"Do you want to go get dinner?" Byron asked.

In no mood to go out for dinner—never mind cooking—Virginia telephoned Hiram, who agreed to bring home Chinese and helped her set out the cartons of take-out on the kitchen table. When she called downstairs for her son, however, he did not answer, and when she walked down to open his bedroom door, he was not there.

The closet door was ruined, the wood splintered where screws had anchored the full-length mirror. The whole thing must have been ripped from the door, she saw. That mirror had been a point of pride, and Virginia felt anger building in her as she pushed open the walk-in closet. The ruined pieces of the mirror were all over the floor, kicked inside hastily by the look of it. The glass had been broken into dozens and dozens of shards and the empty frame lay separately, cracked in the middle.

§

"What did you do to your hand?" Byron asked.

Settled into the passenger seat, Duncan held his hand between his legs and hoped against logic that Byron wouldn't notice. But that didn't happen.

"It's just cut."

"It's cut?"

Byron pulled his parent's car over onto the gravel shoulder and stopped.

"It's fine. I wrapped a t-shirt around it."

"You wrapped a t-shirt around it?"

Duncan wished his friend would shut up for a minute.

"There's quite a bit of blood, but the cuts aren't serious."

"The cuts aren't serious?"

"Stop repeating what I say."

"Stop being an asshole and show me the hand."

Now that her attention was drawn to it, Virginia saw that there was quite a bit of blood: streaked onto the shards of broken mirror, smudged onto the closet doorknob, dragged across the beige berber. The first scenario that flashed through her mind was a suicide–Duncan slicing at his wrist with a long shard, the edges of the glass cutting into the flesh of his gripped hand–but the image was, of course, illogical. Where was the body? She had to assume that the mess in the closet was no more than a sudden outburst, the kind that young men in the throes of exaggerated emotion can be prone to. Embarrassed, he'd probably just shoved the mess in the closet and left. But where was he now? That damn separate entrance had been a bad idea all along.

Upstairs, she listened as Hiram got on the telephone to Madeline's parents.

"No, I don't know if he's there or not. That's why I'm calling. Yes, I know he and Madeline are no longer dating. Perhaps, however, she can tell me where he might be. Can you please put your daughter on the telephone? Yes, thank you."

Her husband's voice stayed reasonable throughout the phone call, which should not have surprised Virginia at all. He'd always had restraint. Thanking Madeline, Hiram said goodbye and dialed Byron's house.

"You really are an asshole, you know."

After getting a look at Duncan's hand, Byron announced that the wounds weren't serious. One cut on his right hand might leave a scar by the thumb, but that was probably the worst of it. No need for the emergency room. They wound up at a booth in Denny's instead.

"Didn't I say you needed to set some ground rules?"

Over pancakes, they talked about their upcoming summer jobs and university–Byron was off to Queen's but Duncan was staying home and commuting downtown to the St. George campus, where his mother studied–and over bottomless coffees, they talked about their shared adolescence. At eighteen years old, Duncan and Byron felt as if adolescence had been a different era, one that could be considered with nostalgia and at great length. If they'd noticed the restaurant tables and booths around them emptying out, they would have been more aware of how late it was getting, and if Byron had known how his friend had left the house abruptly, he would have suggested a call home, but the two were engrossed in conversation, belabouring their shared past.

Although she said she'd never be able to sleep, Virginia let Hiram lead her to bed shortly after one in the morning. He had a nine o'clock conference call, and she was meeting with her department advisor to finalize her thesis defense committee at ten.

"You can get some rest even if you don't sleep right away."

Byron's parents hadn't been sure where her son was, but they'd given Byron the car, so the chances were pretty good that he was with Duncan. Virginia suggested she should maybe call the police station, but she knew the idea was foolish even as she said it.

"I'm just worried and angry, so I feel helpless," she said.

They ate the cold Chinese food, Hiram filling the silence with small talk about the upcoming summer and the chances of getting away to a cottage for a week or so. After, she wrapped the leftovers while Hiram sneaked downstairs with the hand vacuum and a garbage bag, so she wouldn't have to deal with the mess in her son's room.

In bed, they lay quietly until Hiram told her not to worry.

"Duncan will come into his own, on his own."

Tired, Virginia let her mind relax and decided that her husband was right once again. Her last thought before giving into sleep was that she needed to invest less in her son.

After three unsuccessful auditions that he attributed to a wavering confidence, Duncan's first role at the University of Toronto was as Jean in *Miss Julie*. With one set and three actors, the play was a small production in the studio theatre, but he threw himself into rehearsals all the same. Now that he and Madeline Nichol were back together, he had someone to run lines with again, and Duncan was certain he could pull off the role of a manservant crazed with lust and affection, even though it was quite different from the everyman roles he'd always gone for in high school. During the one week of performances, Duncan's mother was out of town—a chance to present a conference paper in Winnipeg on Genetic Predisposition and Identity Development that she could hardly turn down—but Hiram came to closing night, and afterwards, they went out for celebratory drinks.

As he had in high school, Duncan spent a disproportionate amount of his energy at university on rehearsals and school productions. Whenever his grades in a required history of theatre and dramatic literature course fell below a C, he would drop the class, putting it off to a future semester. After five and a half years of university, he hadn't yet earned enough credits for a degree, and he saw little reason to continue.

Over these same years, the privacy that came along with the separate entrance grew, and some weeks, he could go three and four days without seeing his mother and stepfather. During summer vacations, Hiram managed to get Duncan paid internships at his firm, but even then, they worked in different parts of the office and seldom crossed paths. He continued to see Madeline on and off until his fourth year of school, but by then, he'd met a number of women and had learned that what he shared with Madeline wasn't as unique as he'd once believed. First, there was Kendra Margaret, the set decorator in his third-year directing class. Then, Anne Victoria in the Art of Comedy. Lee May, Paula Maya, and Leslie Miriam.

"Why is it you always date women with two first names?" Byron asked.

His friend called from Kingston every once in a while, but over time, their friendly conversations grew shorter, becoming no more than ten-minute exchanges of information. The last Duncan heard, Byron had begun medical school and was dating someone from a study group. Their final conversation gave him the idea for a stage name, however, and thereafter, Duncan Todd auditioned under the pseudonym Todd Duncan.

After he left university, his mother stopped attending his performances altogether, but Duncan continued to believe that if he got a big enough role, she would see it. Throughout his twenties and into his thirties, Todd Duncan must have attended over a thousand auditions–for everything from film and television to fringe festival plays, dinner theatre productions, local commercials, and talking books. On the day of his thirty-fifth birthday, he reviewed his resume and saw that his only credit of note for over a year was a part in the Heron Gate Barn's dinner production of *Arsenic and Old Lace,* and he saw little point in going on.

Through most of those years, he was supporting himself with temporary administrative positions. It was employment that he had experience in after his summer jobs at Hiram's law firm, but not work he'd ever considered a career. When he read of an office manager opening in the municipal offices in Belleville, though, he reconsidered and relocated. After Toronto, the city was slight and a bit too much on the rural side, but Duncan eventually grew used to the limitations. After all, how many movie theatres, restaurants, and stores did one really need? With the internet, Duncan found he spent more and more time at home, anyway, reconnecting with Byron, who was living in Vancouver and working as an emergency room doctor, and with Madeline, who was married and a mother of two in Calgary. Twice a year, Duncan made his way to Toronto for a visit, and once a month or so, either he or his mother telephoned. The calls never lasted long, and afterwards, Duncan tended to be gloomy. Though he couldn't have put his finger on any one specific moment, their relationship had changed significantly at some point in time.

CANADA COACH 2-21,
MONTREAL TO OTTAWA

Rupert Peillard sat on the lowered toilet seat in the rear of Canada Coach 2-21, and Stephan Deviller leaned against the bolted door. Passing between them Peillard's second-to-last and then last joint, the two men laughed. Although a wet clump of brown paper towel and a possibly used Kleenex tissue sat on the floor of the cramped washroom, and although the blue antiseptic water of the toilet sloshed noisily with the sway of the moving bus, neither the old man nor the young man noticed their unhygienic surroundings. Further, if they had noticed, they wouldn't have been at all annoyed, for in addition to Peillard's marijuana, they had earlier warmed themselves with a bottle of Martinique sugarcane rum while waiting in the downtown Montreal terminal for the 11:15 to Ottawa.

Outside of the washroom, the bus was moving westward along highway four seventeen at one hundred and five kilometres—at that moment passing the exit ramp to country road nine—and the lovely sight passing by in front of the bus windows was something to see: a nighttime landscape of successive and seemingly endless banks of deciduous trees in April. The rain had stopped an hour earlier, but the needles of the evergreens remained wet and picked up the light from the moon. Unlike a number of other passengers on Canada Coach 2-21, however, Peillard and Deviller were not inclined to admire the province's rural scenery because they had met but hours earlier and were still experiencing the selfless generosity that only a newly-formed friendship can provide.

Yesterday, after a night in a shelter by the old port, Peillard woke on a bottom bunk in a room with seven men he'd never met before. It was still dark out but the light from the window revealed the old man's temporary roommates. Like himself, most of the sleeping bundles under the grey wool blankets were unshaven and had been unshaven for weeks, and although he knew it was unkind to think, the small room held the smell of unwashed men. One man, sleeping on his side and curled in on himself, was younger by half than Peillard and the others. He couldn't have been more than twenty-five or twenty-six, and he was sleeping soundly, most likely unaccustomed to a night in a mission bed. His backpack sat on the floor propped up against the bunk, and a small luggage clip-lock held the top flap down, idiotically signaling the probable value of the contents. Peillard stretched out his leg and hooked the bag with his foot, dragging it to his own bunk, where one solid tug ripped open the side seam and revealed a Ziploc baggie containing four marijuana cigarettes. Peillard rolled the plastic bag into the sleeve of his sweater, and just as the sky was turning a light morning grey, he slipped out the side door of the shelter. It was bitter cold and raining, as it had been on and off for the entire week, but in Chinatown Peillard purchased two sticks of fried dough from a bakery where he sat and read through an abandoned *Gazzette* for the entire morning. Afterward, he walked in the drizzle and to keep warm, stamped his feet while he gazed at the elaborate store displays. Letting his mind wander, he imagined he was actually window-shopping, but the game grew tiring and he grew tired, and so Peillard stopped to rest his feet on a concrete bench in Rutherford Park. Once seated, he realized that despite the chilly air, he had started to sweat beneath his coat, and the sweat was quickly turning him cold. Peillard rubbed his hands against each other, and for reasons he could not put together, he thought of his first wife. She had been the first of three, and even though he hadn't seen her in fifteen years, she remained his favourite. Celia was the only wife with whom he agreed to have a child. The specific memory that came to him at that moment was of waking her for a waffle and egg breakfast in bed. It must have been on her birthday or an anniversary or some other day of significance because even Peillard would admit that he wasn't one to pamper a loved one too too much. On the breakfast tray, he remembered, he'd placed three ramekins of preserves beside Celia's plate. One orange-pineapple marmalade, one banana chutney, and one more that Peillard wished for the life of him he could remember. While he tried to keep warm and tried to pin down a decade-and-a-half old memory, his distraction was such that he stopped rubbing his hands and was unknowingly holding them still in front of himself in an unnatural tableau. To a passing observer, he would have appeared stunned frozen as if by a weapon of science fiction. Who knows how long he would have remained immobile if not for Deviller's voice of concern.

"What the hell's with you, pal?"

Asked to leave his mother and stepfather's condominium apartment the previous evening, Deviller had thought he would pay for a hostel bed for the night and then leave Montreal for Gatineau where his older brother had an extra room in the basement. Once at the Royal Bank ATM, however, the young man decided not to squander away his limited cash on a night's shelter, and he remained in the dry bank kiosk, where he nodded off asleep on the floor. What he dreamt of was his thirteenth birthday. He'd had a bowling party, and for the first time, his now estranged father had allowed him to invite both girls and boys. In the dream, he sat at the head of the table in Magic Lane's party room surrounded by friends from his grade eight gifted class. They laughed about their Language Arts teacher's speech impediment and they shared their ideas for the upcoming Science Fair. For sure one of their classmates would win the Science Fair; of the entire school, Deviller and his gifted class friends held the most promise. When he opened his eyes, the fluorescent lights of the kiosk immediately reminded him where he was and that he was alone. His brother would not return home from the construction site he managed until late in the evening, and so, for the bulk of the morning and early afternoon, Deviller passed the hours in an Indigo megastore. For the most part, the bookstore staff left him to himself and he read through the introduction and first three chapters of a nonfiction bestseller that simplified game theory for a general audience. The reading excited Deviller, but his enthusiasm made him restless, and a little after two in the afternoon, he decided that despite the drizzle outside, a walk was just what was needed to calm his mind. He walked eastward and stared down at his feet against the wet cement sidewalks. In less than a month, he imagined, cafe tables and chairs would fill the wide sidewalks and people would be chatting and friendly. For now, though, his fellow pedestrians walked by him silently with their hands jammed in their pockets and their heads tucked down into their overcoats. People should be less guarded, Deviller thought, and so when he passed by Rutherford Park and saw Peillard as immobile as granite, he voiced his concern.

"What the hell's with you, pal?"

Shaken loose from unconsciousness, the older man turned his head up to the younger. Wordlessly, Peillard slid to one end of his bench and allowed Deviller to sit. Peillard introduced himself, and then, to his own surprise, explained his sudden memory of Celia. Deviller nodded in understanding and—also unexpected—told of his out-of-the-blue dream of grade eight. From a *dépanneur*, the younger man purchased a domestic red wine, and back on the park bench, they shared the bottle and talked. They spoke of past homes and past jobs and past loves and near-loves, and when they had exhausted topics of the past, the younger man suggested the older travel to

Ottawa with him. He would front Peillard money for the bus ticket, and Deviller's older brother would probably be able to find work for both of them. With summer coming, construction crews would need dozens of extra hands, and it wasn't as if experience or references were required. Passing an SAQ on the way to the bus depot, the younger man purchased a second–and stronger–bottle of alcohol, and slouched in departure chairs near gate twelve, the older man removed the plastic baggie from the sleeve of his sweater. They smoked the first two joints in the station's basement washroom, but it wasn't until they were well across the Quebec-Ontario border that they decided to smoke the second-to-last and last.

Of course, the ceiling, floor, and corners of the passenger bus restroom were not airtight, and the marijuana skunk seeped into the interior of the bus, drifting forward from the rear and making its way to each of the nighttime travellers. Each and every passenger identified the distinct smell immediately, and although none voiced their thoughts aloud, each of them had distinct feelings and opinions about the situation and what should be done about it.

AARON WELLS Tell the driver. It's the smart thing to do, and it is his job. Canada Coach must have some sort of set procedures for dealing with this sort of problem, and the driver is paid to follow those procedures.

DONALD HARVEY Of course you tell the driver, but after you tell the driver, he is obliged to radio his supervisor and the police will probably meet the bus somewhere up ahead on the highway. It'd have to be the OPP's responsibility, I imagine. Pulling up on the side of the dirt shoulder would be too dangerous, so they would almost certainly tell the driver to exit the highway. The gas bar just before Casselman would be the most sensible place. I don't imagine these two guys would give the police much trouble or resistance, so getting them off the bus and into the back of the cruiser wouldn't take any time at all. The only delay would be the passengers, really. Each of us would have to give some sort of statement as witnesses. In the end, our two-hour trip from Montreal could turn into three or four hours. Not worth the trouble.

MORTON VALLE At one time I might of said you talk to the two men direct. I'd of said you just can't go around keeping your mouth shut when you see when people do wrong. Do that, not only does the wrong continue, but you also grow timid and weak on the inside. Let someone push you around and soon enough you start believing that they got the right. So yes, at one point in the past, I would of stood up for myself. Car sneaked into the spot I was backing into, I said something. Guy threw litter in my neighborhood, I said something. Lady behind the diner counter was rude, I said something. But then I got punched in ear last summer. Fellow was driving too fast for the supermarket parking lot, and I told him so and he punched me in the ear. He didn't back down at all. Just punched me in the ear.

ERIC ROSE I got on from the airport pickup at Trudeau so I didn't see these two drinking in the bus station downtown. Not that their behaviour surprises me. Walk a few blocks around Montreal and you'll hear drunken or drugged mumblings on every second corner. Sure it's like that all over, but Montreal always seems worse. As if such behaviour is part of their distinct culture.

STEPHANIE WRIGHT Smell is the most dominant sense for triggering memory. That's what my mother always said. Mother didn't finish junior high, and she held fast onto this piece of information like an uneducated person will. She brought the fact into conversations even when it didn't at all fit, and she was ready to argue her position if challenged. Not that she wasn't intelligent. Just insecure. The pot triggers a number of memories for me. Outdoor concerts. High school dances and we were all crowded around outside by the fire exit. University residence, of course. But the strongest memory marijuana smoke calls up is of my mother. I was with Samuel Gruenberg then, so the memory must come from grade eleven or twelve, and we were in the basement. Normally, my parents returned from work at six, so Sam and I weren't worried, but of course my mother had a head cold that same day and took the afternoon off. She most likely smelled the marijuana drifting up from the basement through the vents, or else she heard Sam and me giggling like fools. What was unusual was that she didn't yell or cry melodramatically as she usually did when I acted out as a child. She just looked at me, turned around and made her way back upstairs. I recall turning to Sam and shrugging or laughing, and that was when I heard my mother fall on the stairs. They were these narrow, steep wooden stairs and really should have been replaced. My mother's nose and mouth were bloody but she hadn't broken anything. I felt awful of course, and to make matters worse, my mother only told my father that she'd been clumsy and slipped for no reason whatsoever.

ARNOLD PETRIE This house proposes that provincial governments regulate the sale and use of marijuana. That was one of the season's topics last year when I was a junior. I can't remember exactly what the wording was but there was a marijuana topic when I was on the sophomore debate team too. Our school uses the parliamentary system and we don't get to pick proposition or opposition, but I always prefer to defend marijuana. More interesting to argue what you don't personally believe. And there seems to be more research in favour of. After the first and second constructive, we go into a rebuttal round which is when things get real fun. I don't know how I would argue for smoking on a bus, though.

KARINE REBUS Fifteen years I smoked. Players Light king size. Like most everyone, I quit a dozen times before I quit for good. But you know, even though I've been off them for seven years, I feel like I could go back. Something bad happens like my husband dies or one of the kids goes missing, and I can see myself running to the Mac's Milk for a pack first thing. And then my seven years of not smoking wouldn't really be quitting. It'd just be a short interruption in my addiction. And even without any big tragedy, some days are hard. Some days I wonder why everyone isn't on something or other. So I try not to judge.

WAYNE AND COLLEEN BARRIE You know, before the kids were born, we used to take these camping trips to Muskoka. We couldn't afford proper vacations, but we always managed to rent a canoe and borrow a tent from someone or other at least once a year. We'd have a cooler of hotdogs and cold cuts or whatever, and we'd also fish for our meals. At night we'd set up a small fire to do the marshmallows. We always had a little bit of pot with us, and one year we decided it'd be fun to smoke out in the canoe on the water. Everything was fine and fun until we got the giggles and tipped right in. Lucky us, we weren't foolish enough to forget our life preservers so we just floated and bobbed around in the water for a while. Drugs can be dangerous.

DOUGLAS BAXTER The correct procedure in this situation is to radio my supervisor at the Ottawa station and await further instruction. However, if I did this every time someone decided to sneak a cigarette in the washroom, my route would run late two or three times a shift. And although my shift supervisor wouldn't exactly be happy that I overlook these incidents, she wouldn't exactly be happy if I couldn't finish all of my runs.

HARRISON FORESTER I saw them drinking in the bus station, slumped in those blue molded plastic chairs, and not surprisingly, the banks of chairs facing them and behind them were entirely empty. People steer clear, and you cannot really blame them for that. And I'm not so very different at all, but the sight of these two drunken men made me smile. Maybe because one of them is old and one is young. There was something almost encouraging in the sight of them. You know, *I am a human, and so I find nothing human foreign to me.*

When all that remained of the final joint was a stub too short to be held, Stephan Deviller rolled the remains between his fingers and the burning ember fell into the open toilet. *Fsssst.* Rupert Peillard eased open the washroom door with care, for even in his altered state, he half expected disapproving stares from passengers turned around in their seats. When no such stares came, he nodded to the younger man behind him, and balanced against headrests, the two men walked halfway down the aisle and found a pair of seats apart from one another.

Deviller lay on his side, curled in on himself to fit into the two seats, with his feet jammed in between the armrest and the bus sidewall. For the remaining thirty-five minutes of the bus ride, he slept without dreaming, and he woke only when the driver illuminated the interior and requested that passengers remain in their seats until the bus came to a full stop. Upon waking, Deviller thought of his brother and his brother's home, and the thoughts made him smile. Both bulkier and taller than Deviller, Peillard had tried tucking into a fetal position but either his head or feet stuck out into to aisle and he could not find comfort. Settled in against the reclined backrest with his coat draped across him, he was at last able to drift asleep, and like his newfound friend, he too slept without dreaming. At the sound of the driver's voice over the bus speakers, Peillard opened his eyes, and because he was warm, dry, and still under the influence, he smiled. As the driver's tired voice instructed continuing travelers with connections to North Bay to make their way to gate seven, Peillard watched the passengers stand to stretch their stiff arms and legs, remove their duffels and briefcases from the overhead compartments, and queue up obediently to exit Canada Coach 2-21, and across the aisle, he saw the happy expression on the younger man's face.

"You have a good nap?" the older man asked.

Although the question was intended as a caring gesture, he voiced his words of kindness loudly enough for many of the worn-out passengers to overhear. Aaron Wells decided he would ask the driver for his name and then call the Canada Coach head office to complain in the morning. Although irritated, Donald Harvey was distractedly wondering if he should call a cab or walk the four blocks to his hotel, and so he gave neither Peillard nor Deviller much thought. Morton Valle wished he were younger and stronger, because if he had been, he certainly would have given them a piece of his mind. Turning to Stephanie Wright, Eric Rose muttered a comment she thought offensive, but she didn't bother with a response. It wasn't her responsibility to correct everyone she met. Arnold Petrie found Peillard's words interesting and wondered to what extent friendship and compassion can be affected by socio-economic factors. Because she had tried and failed to nap all the way from downtown Montreal, Karine Rebus resented the younger man's ability to sleep. Neither Colleen nor Wayne Barrie heard, for she was at that moment asking her husband whether or not he took his pill before dinner, but he could not recall. Douglas Baxter's shift was soon ending and so his thoughts were occupied by the half hour of paperwork that would finish his workday. Of all the passengers, only Harrison Forester was touched by the older man's obvious fondness for the younger man, and Harrison smiled.

"You have a good nap?"

Fully awake, Deviller stopped smiling. The peacefulness of his sleep vanished. Unbeknownst to Peillard, his voice contained an unexpectedly paternal tone, and for the younger man, such a voice triggered a series of associations and elicited emotions that were too conflicted to sort out at twenty-six years old. Deviller's stomach hurt, and his first thought was to ditch the older man as soon as they exited the bus. Such an act wasn't in his nature, though, and he struggled against his reaction. As if to compensate for his increasing gloom, he purchased both himself and Peillard a coffee from a vending machine in the Ottawa station. Deviller was nearly out of money, and although the coffee probably wouldn't be any good, he said it'd warm them before they headed outside where the rain had once again picked up.

The walk to the brother's house took hours, and as they moved along the bridge and crossed again into Quebec, the sky was turning a light morning grey. They hadn't spoken since the station but each man was thinking of the other. Deviller decided what was best was to let the old man down easy. He would ask his brother to lie and claim that unfortunately the construction site just didn't have enough work for two new hires. Peillard would certainly understand. The construction work would probably pay well enough for the younger man to forget about the bus ticket money. If Peillard stayed in the basement with him an extra night, that'd be all right too. They could, Deviller decided, just drift away from one another.

At that same moment, Peillard too decided that they should part. Crossing the bridge, he couldn't help but see the far stretch of the river east and west. The surface was churned up and chaotic, the rain water colliding with the river water again and again. The sight was lovely really, and it gave Peillard pause. As if viewing himself from above, he saw a man of fifty-seven years holding his overcoat tight to keep warm while wandering in a city he did not know with a companion he did not know, and earlier, he'd crammed himself into a filthy toilet and lounged there casually to smoke stolen drugs. Peillard saw himself as a busload of strangers might. He would, he thought, follow Deviller and rest in the warmth of a home for a few hours, and then, while the younger man slept soundly, he would slip out of the house and be on his way.

COMORBIDITIES

This isn't a story we were meant to hear. But whenever dinner company was in the house, one or more of us would slide out from under our tightly tucked sheets and sneak to the top of the stairs to eavesdrop. When it was all five of us, we huddled together, the older shushing the excited giggles of the younger, and we struggled to listen and understand the conversation floating up from downstairs.

Mother and Father were entertaining for out-of-town guests that they hadn't seen in *for-goodness-knew* how long. The Overmeyers. Mother was connected to the couple from university before she married Father, but he seemed to know them pretty well too. It was hard to make out any one voice at first. Mother and Mrs. Overmeyer cleared the dessert dishes and loaded the dishwasher while Father and Mr. Overmeyer set out the liqueur glasses from the dining room cabinet, and the adult conversation overlapped into one indistinct murmur that was occasionally punctuated by a bark of a laugh. Eventually, though, the din faded and only Mother's voice was left. She was telling a story that had been hidden from us, but her voice had the easy rhythm of a repeated and revised anecdote, and she must have retold it to any number of friends and relatives. The story was about the birth of the last of us and how father had shouted out a profanity in the delivery room.

"The first time and last time he has used such language in front of me," Mother said.

This was at the end of her fifth and final pregnancy, which had been complicated and had seemed much longer than the preceding four. Extra appointments with our family GP and with the obstetrician, as well as one late night race to the emergency in Willowdale General. Ultrasounds at three, four, eight and nine months, and after such a troubled journey to the delivery room, our normally obliging father was unnerved when the obstetrician asked Mother why she'd stopped pushing right in the middle of labour.

"I didn't know I had," she told the Overmeyers.

Mother had not admitted to this in the delivery room, however, for pushing wasn't the only problem. For some unknown reason, the vision in her left eye had turned milky and she was overcome by fatigue, and while fatigue during childbirth is hardly uncommon, this sudden exhaustion was isolated to the left side of her body. Something wasn't right. She shook herself, and at last, admitted that she thought she had been pushing. The doctor turned and muttered something indistinct to one of the nurses in the room, a secret communication that was followed by a bustle and the repositioning of pediatric personnel and unidentifiable medical equipment.

"A real hullabaloo," Mother said.

The commotion was all quite distressing, and whatever had gone wrong with Mother's body, it was far too much for Father. Thirty-nine weeks of urine and blood tests, clinic waiting rooms, and warnings of an unspecified danger, and thus, his worry and frustration and helplessness peaked in the delivery room.

"Fuck this noise."

The Overmeyers chortled, and Mother allowed herself a laugh as well.

"Mind you, it wasn't quite as amusing at the time."

Because she had trained and worked as a registered nurse's assistant herself, Mother knew that the assembly of doctors and nurses would ignore the outburst. Inappropriate behaviour is overlooked in hospitals on a daily basis. Holding Father's hand tighter, she encouraged him with soft words and reminded him that it would all be over soon. The waiting was the worst of it, and the worst of it was nearly behind them. At this point in her life, she still possessed patience and tolerance, and in the end, the obstetrician employed a pair of metal forceps, and the last of us was born into the world.

While Mother and Father calmed down, the doctor performed the kind of examinations all newborns go through. Colouration, temperature, breathing, blood pressure. He correctly concluded that the faint forceps marks on the skin above the temples were the only damage. Nothing more than cosmetic, and if they didn't fade with age, the marks would be covered by hair eventually anyway. Father stood up and held out his arms, but one of the pediatric nurses waved him back down. The last thing they needed was his fainting and taking a tumble in all the excitement. There would be plenty of time to hold the baby later.

"Turned out fine," Mother concluded to the Overmeyers.

As told to the dinner guests, the birth story ended as all birth stories should—exhausted mother cradling a healthy baby and embarrassed father apologizing for such poor manners—and the Overmeyers laughed again.

The happy murmuring of conversation restarted, Mother's individual voice fading once again into the overlapping bustle. We were tired by then, so one by one, we stood up from the top of the stairs, and one by one, we returned to our shared bedrooms. We climbed into the toddler bed that we had already outgrown. We crawled into the trundle bed that squeaked. We mounted the ladder of the bunk bed and heaved ourselves in. We fell asleep as soon as we closed our eyes, and we stayed up whispering about swearing and Father and Mother.

After the delivery room difficulties, the obstetrician and our family doctor insisted upon test after test, and Mother was referred out to a succession of specialists around North York. These appointments must have amounted to quite a few scheduling headaches. Father had managed less than two weeks off from his accounting firm, Mother was once again at home with a newborn, and on top of shuttling us back and forth from sports and clubs and extracurriculars, our parents and their already hectic schedules were further burdened with visits to the pediatrician, the lactation consultant, and the public health nurse. With a new child, Mother and Father simply had no time to worry about why her body had acted erratically during childbirth, and busy as we were with growing up, we hardly noticed at all. We were teething. We had soccer and softball. We had a crush on Tom Baker, who sat two desks down in French and was on the Gauss Math Team with us. We had a four-block paper route delivering *the Toronto Star.*

And ultimately, the tests never led anywhere conclusive, the specialists never specific about the cause of the trouble. Mother was losing her baby weight and her body was feeling like itself again. With no recurrence, the momentary problems during childbirth could be chalked up to just another of the human body's oddities. A harmless episode to share with dinner guests. Like an alarming lump that appears under an armpit only to disappear inexplicably the following week, mother's blurred vision and the weakness could be pushed from her mind, entirely dismissed and effortlessly disregarded.

§

When the last of us was done with diapers, past preschool and settled into senior kindergarten, Mother grew restless and thought about a return to the workforce. Her last job at a walk-in clinic in Richmond Hill was long gone unfortunately, and her replacement, it turned out, was a provincially licensed nurse with a four year degree in chemistry and microbiology. When a string of applications produced but one unsatisfying interview, Mother rightfully worried about her inadequate RNA qualifications. Father assured her that his accountant's position provided more than enough to cover the mortgage of our crowded townhouse, but with five of us and five possible tuitions looming, Mother lowered her expectations and took a position at the BallyCliffe Retirement home. For two full years, she fed and bathed the elderly who could not always feed and bathe themselves. She helped them dress, she changed their bed sheets, and she gave them their medications. After all that time home with children, adult conversation was a welcome change, and the old folks at BallyCliffe were pretty well-informed, she said. They read every section of the newspaper, and they had opinions they weren't afraid to defend. Of course, the patients also talked of their grandchildren and Mother also talked of us.

We couldn't get the hang of subtracting three digit numerals. We hated the school librarian Ms. Seagull who was mean about overdue books. We'd developed a crush on our Spanish tutor. We wished we didn't have to share bedrooms and we complained about it all the time. We came home from after-school club and she could smell cigarette smoke on our clothes. We were darlings all the same.

One morning near the end of July, Mother and one of her favourite residents, Mrs. Thompson, were chatting while changing the bedding together. Mother liked Mrs. Thompson because, as she said, the old woman was opinionated beyond belief and stubborn like the dickens. Mrs. Thompson refused most assistance from the BallyCliffe staff, calling such assistance mollycoddling, and only accepted Mother's help when it was disguised as conversation and a friendly visit. As long as the two of them chatted away about this and that, the old woman didn't have to admit to any limitations. And so they were making the bed together and Mother was mock-complaining about all the ridiculous arts and crafts friendship bracelets we brought home from summer Y camp when a milky film clouded the vision in her right eye. Her voice stopped in mid-sentence and she blinked quickly as if she might chase away the nuisance, but she could not. It got worse and she couldn't see out of her right eye.

Mother's disloyal vision returned some three hours later. After signing out of BallyCliffe, she reached our father by telephone and assured him she could get to hospital by herself. No, an ambulance certainly wasn't necessary–there was a direct line phone to Beck Taxi right there in the retirement home lobby–and no, she didn't want him to leave work to sit with her. Someone needed to pick us up from afterschool club and the sitter's, and it was Wednesday, so that meant Spanish Tutoring and Sea Otter Swim. The leftover lasagna style hamburger helper on the second shelf of the fridge could be reheated, and there was a boil-in-the-bag thing of corn niblets in the freezer. We all ate the corn, she assured him.

"Who knows how long the hospital wait will be," she said.

The wait was an hour as it turned out, just enough time to register at the front desk and flip awkwardly through a leftover *MacLean's*, which she'd had to hold awkwardly on her left side in order to compensate for the blind spot on her right. An odd reading experience, she said. Out of reflex or habit or whatever, she kept turning her head, and anyone passing by would have thought her a mad woman. Fortunately, emergency rooms are full of mad people and most mind their own business. Midway through a book review of some sort of espionage thriller or other, she noticed a small light flutter in her right eye, as if someone far away were walking toward her with a lantern, and as she rubbed at the eye, her blindness gave way to a cloudiness that slowly cleared and once again became sight.

"And the kicker?" She told Father. "The admin nurse called my name not five minutes later."

Her flippancy was pretence, of course. She was making jest where there was none, and Father wasn't having any of it. He said he was going to call our family doctor tomorrow and he was going to come along for each and every test and examination. He was going to be there for every doctor appointment and follow up, he was going to be there to hear for himself what the ophthalmologist and the neurologist had to say, and he was not about to stay home with us while she was going through this.

"The children can look after each other well enough."

Seen in women three to four times more often than in men, Multiple Sclerosis is an autoimmune disease in which the body's immune system damages the axons and myelin sheaths located in the white matter of the brain. The first phase of the condition, relapsing-remitting MS, appears in patients between twenty to forty years of ages and can last anywhere between ten to thirty years' time. Because attacks occur in the brain, symptoms are unpredictable and can be as varied as depression, lack of coordination, blindness, memory failure, muscle weakness, sexual difficulties, bladder problems, and incontinence.

The MRI revealed lesions, flecks spotted across the surface of the scan, and the neurologist came back with a definitive answer, the specific and conclusive diagnosis that had eluded earlier specialists. It gave our parents pause and made Mother reexamine past events with new knowledge and insight. Her on-and-off dizziness for those three days leading up to their wedding, her fatigue during their honeymoon through Norway, Sweden, and Finland, and all that trouble she'd had remembering names at her fifth high school reunion. Could these incidents be retroactively explained by her illness? Our father tried his best to comfort her. Were not all brides dizzy at some point? Were not package tours exhausting for everyone? And the school really should have prepared name tags for the alumni.

"Oh, God," she said. "When I dropped the baby?"

She was referring to a day when the last of us was fourteen months, balanced on her hip while she loaded the stroller with sand toys for the park. Without warning, her muscles had failed her. The drop was no more than a couple of feet and the diaper absorbed most the impact, but it set off a peal of wailing that lasted all the way home.

"Every child gets dropped on its head at least once," Father said.

When Mother and Father sat us down to share and discuss the diagnosis, we had a lot of questions. Did this mean Mother couldn't come see us perform as a wise man in the Cub Scouts Nativity Play? Did this mean she couldn't help us practice driving even though we'd worked so hard to pass the 365 permit test? Did this mean she wouldn't be able to take us to the library to meet our Spanish tutor? Did this mean she would die like Nana Varley? The symptoms might come and go at some unnamed point in the future, she said, and yes, the unpredictability was frightening, but we didn't have to be frightened.

"A disseminated sclerosis can affect any aspect of the nervous system at any time abruptly and without warning."

She was repeating the unreal words of the neurologist, but she kindly did not include the phrase he had callously added. Unpredictable changes, he had said, were par for the course. His best advice was to take it easy. Avoid strenuous tasks for prolonged periods. Cut back on hours at work. Consider a job that wasn't as physically demanding as BallyCliffe.

Over the next decade and a half until her death, what was par for the course was vision loss. What was par for the course was hearing loss. What was par for the course was a worsening and eventually chronic fatigue. Loss of function in the left arm, left leg, and both legs. Two seizures. Occasional, yet severe bouts of depression. And at the very end, the unkindest of amalgams–deaf, blind, and confined to a wheeled chair.

What was par for the course was Braille. What was par for the course was an electric wheelchair. What was par for the course was a move to a suburban ranch bungalow without stairs. Tactile finger spelling for the deaf and blind. Periodically–at times when the severity and unpredictability of the symptoms seemed particularly cruel and unusual–our tired mother and father had to shake their heads and wonder if there were any worse malady.

Of course there is.

There was one full year between that first diagnosis and the first protracted symptom. Because they were readers, our parents used much of that time to do what readers do; they ordered library books and tried to learn what they could about the illness, vainly hoping that knowledge and information would or could in some way help. Medical books with cryptic terminology and unnatural syntax. Handbooks for chronic patients that included recipes and tips on reducing life's stresses. Self help books with vague advice disguised as information. Our parents read indiscriminately that year.

It was also a year during which we learned to balance a three-speed without hands for a block and a half. A year during which we mastered the subtraction of three and four digit numerals and moved onto our multiplication tables. A year during which our Spanish tutor betrayed our heart by walking hand in hand with his older grade eleven girlfriend through the mall food court right in front of all our friends.

We were brought out of our natural childhood self involvement just before the Easter long weekend when her first protracted symptom came. Late into the Thursday night or early early Good

Friday morning, Mother lost her sight. She had closed her eyes and had gone to sleep, and then she had awoken up to a dark blur. Both eyes this time. Reaching through the bed sheets, she found Father's sleeping form and told him the news. Stay still, stay in bed. That was his instinctual advice, but she would have none of it. Did he expect her to stay in bed all day or all weekend? Had he forgotten the Easter holiday? Did staying in bed make the least bit of sense? Defeated, our father agreed, and with his help, she made her way down to the kitchen nook, settling in there for much of the long weekend. What she saw was nothing more than shadow against light. It was only when we spoke that we were at all distinct, though none of us much knew what to say.

In later years, when we were adults and more adept at empathy, we would shudder at the thoughts and uncertainty that must have beset her for that entire long weekend. She wouldn't have wanted to believe that her vision problems were permanent but that must have occurred to her. She must have wondered how much of her life and how much of our lives she would miss. She must have wondered how long she should wait until she called BallyCliffe. She must have gone to sleep Friday, Saturday, and Sunday night hoping to see once again, and each morning she must have awoken in alarm as she rediscovered her loss all over again. When she and Father spoke, they focused on immediate concerns. With sick days and vacation days, she could postpone her resignation until mid-May, and maybe that would be enough time for her sight to return. Maybe those few weeks would be enough time for this first protracted symptom to abate. Maybe this first symptom in the relapsing and remitting phase was short term. It was not.

Entirely disregarding our mother's illness, Easter came, and we went downstairs Sunday morning to see what the Easter Bunny that only one of us still believed in had left behind, his trail of foil-wrapped chocolate eggs and coloured jelly beans in strategic locations hidden around the townhouse. Along the edge of the massive stereo cabinet, behind the vertical blinds, under each of the chesterfield cushions. The younger of us were momentarily able to forget Mother and grow excited as we hunted, filling the basket in a hurry and boasting that we would find even more than last year, but as the hiding spots became more obscure, the search slowed. Under the floor vents, inside the loveseat pillowslips, on the upper edge of the frames holding our family portraits.

"Maybe I should help look?" Mother suggested.

The stress of the previous days had taken its toll.

"No, really," she said. "Let me help. I could creep around on the carpet on my hands and knees."

She proceeded to do so.

As with many of their many disagreements, quarrels, and fights over the subsequent years, the argument that followed was more-or-less one-sided. Father spoke to appease and calm as best he could, but it was a counter-productive strategy that only frustrated Mother more. Eventually, we were sent to the basement to entertain ourselves with television, foil-wrapped chocolate eggs and coloured jelly beans.

While unpredictable symptoms during the relapsing-remitting phase cease for occasional physical relief, the chronic nature of Multiple Sclerosis means that symptoms may reappear as abruptly and as they disappear, making stability in work and home life difficult to maintain. For many, a professional career is impossible, and when work is possible, a flexible employer is indispensable. At home, the patient's natural and ongoing feelings of anger and depression can complicate family dynamics and structure, altering romantic or spousal relationships as well as parent and child connections.

§

It may well be that her first blind Easter did not unfold in the exact manner that we remember, for we do not always agree upon the past. One of us claims Mother didn't pull that crawling stunt until years later. One of us claims Mother wasn't blind when she hunted around on the floor, but in a wheelchair and on depression meds; she actually crawled out of her chair, and that was why we were all so upset. Some of us think her eyesight was gone for no more than six months that first time. Some of us think her eyesight didn't return for nearly two years more. Our memories cannot be wholly reliable; they are too often distorted, too often contradictory, and too often conveniently associated with family Easters, Christmases, Thanksgivings, and birthdays. Maybe it doesn't matter.

What we know for sure: her vacation and sick time from BallyCliffe ran out, and thereafter, Mother alternated between periodic work and LTD until the time of her death. Also, there were many visitors to the house during that first period of blindness. The loud Scottish woman from the MS Society whose accent was cartoonishly thick. The Public Health nurse who always wore the same yellow cardigan. The youth pastor from the United Church who had a left eye that wandered. The only name that sticks with us is Zahra, an impossibly tiny and effortlessly kind woman from the CNIB. With home visits every day, Mother learned to read Braille from Zahra during that first long stretch of blindness.

"As good a time as any to catch up on your reading," she said.

Her deadpan got our mother laughing, and we often heard their happy voices overlapping one another when we returned home from school. As we were taught to greet all visitors, we would go into the dining room before fleeing up to our room or down to the basement, and we saw the thick scraps of a heavy Braille paper that littered the dining room table, where Mother moved from letters, to words, sentences, and whole paragraphs. The sluggish progress was sad to witness during those brief after-school minutes. Eventually, though, we returned home to find Zahra and Mother reading together aloud from identically oversized books, both of them slowly tracing their fingers over lines of raised text. With little else to occupy her late into the evening, Mother would return alone to the dining room table after dinner, using her punch tool and a hinged metal template to practice writing. Once she'd relearned basic literacy, she ordered translated Braille magazines from the CNIB, and we remember a single issue of *MacLean's* that came in four volumes, each one the size of a Toronto phonebook.

While we can now hardly believe we held such concerns, Mother's first protracted symptom meant any number of additional losses for us. It meant we had to muster through long division and fractions on our own. It meant our annual camp and canoe trip to Bon Echo was indefinitely postponed. It meant we chose not to sign up for soccer and softball because ferrying us to and from practices were unnecessary inconveniences. It meant that even though our middle school crush returned our attentions and we'd made out in the gym stairwell, we would never mention him at home. It meant that now that we had a driver's license, we were expected to take Mother to the IGA and the Shopper's Drug Mart and the Richmond Hill Plaza whenever she wished.

Outdoors, she used a white cane that ingeniously folded down like a bungeed tent pole, but in the market and in the mall, Mother insisted on leaving the white cane tucked away in her purse, preferring to take our elbow or hand or shoulder, a sight that could not help but make others stare. Men, women, children, and whole families of shoppers stared and quickly turned away as Mother read aloud from her Braille shopping and to-do lists. We were as embarrassed by our parents as any adolescent is, but we learned to be ashamed of our embarrassment too. And the stares of the shoppers that were the hardest were not the secret, quick glances but the sustained looks of esteem, the looks that told us we were dutiful accompanying our blind mother and admiration was due. We knew better. The feeling was worse later on with the wheelchair.

No matter the length of that first symptom, it was far too long not to see one's children, and when we now look upon on our growing sons and daughters, we cannot imagine bearing such an absence. We shot up three inches in a single summer. We started shaving. We hit puberty and wrecked our complexion. We grew a van dyke. We went through three different unwise hairstyles.

The week before Thanksgiving, she woke up early and stared at the stucco ceiling of the master bedroom. At first, the sight made no sense at all. A greying inverted moonscape, the ceiling was only slightly distinguishable from the fog she had been living with for months, but then, her mind adjusted, and she understood that that she was seeing. Gratitude hit her in a sudden rush, she said, and it was a gratitude that lasted days and days, the emotion intensified by the Thanksgiving holiday. She shed tears watching the oldest of us carve the turkey. She shed tears greeting us when returned from our first semester of university. She shed tears settling down on the chesterfield beside us to watch television for the first time in a year.

Her thoughts must have been complicated by the possibility of a relapse, of course, but this did not occur to us until later. This protracted symptom had been the first, and we did not yet fully understand the cruel and unusual punishment of her unpredictable illness. We were happy and young enough to be incautious about happiness, taken in by our own false sense of security and taken by surprise when she lost her hearing some three months later.

§

Decades later, long after we have stopped mourning our mother's death daily, our cheated sense of security will remain and will have evolved within each of us. We will be cautious in parenthood, will refuse our own children a backyard trampoline, will not allow contact sports, will discourage team sports, will buy homes in cul-de-sacs with little traffic, will grow to see the automobiles as a threat to safety and despise their very invention. We will be reckless in romance, will have trouble forming long-term attachments, will sleep with married women, will marry and divorce the first woman that comes along. The youngest of us–those of us who could not remember a time before the unpredictably illness–will distrust all forms of stability and certainty. We will never believe in any religious system or the possibility of a higher power. We will not believe that hard work leads to success, that knowledge is power, or that persistence is rewarded. We will put no stock in good luck or bad luck. We will not be taken aback by dreadful news of the day, or the worst of human nature, or any of the world's rot. We will buy a great deal of insurance.

As she had with Zahra from the CNIB, Mother accepted a volunteer from the North York Bob Rumble to teach her what she needed to learn. The young man who came to tutor her in American Sign Language was polite and patient, but overly optimistic, smiling in an exaggerated way every visit to the house. Greeting us after school, he grinned as he spoke and signed all of his words with gleeful sweeping gestures.

"I suspect he's born again," Mother said.

After three weeks of finger spelling and vocabulary building at the dining room table, Mother canceled his visits. It turned out she'd picked up lip reading without much effort, and so what was really the point of learning ASL? She didn't say, but years later,

Father later told us she missed Zahra's friendship, and the boy's forced cheer made her feel even more low.

Later, when symptoms overlapped one another, and Mother lost both her sight and her hearing at once, no volunteers came to the house at all. She would not let them. We returned to the house and found her sitting in the kitchen nook chain smoking. She did not much want to talk at all, but when it was necessary to communicate, we traced out letters, words, and short ungrammatical sentences on her palm, the process painfully slow.

"And bloody ridiculous," Father said.

He was less patient with depression than with other symptoms, and at the library, he found a book on tactile finger spelling and common word abbreviations for the deaf and blind. As a language, it was inefficient, but the twenty-six letters of the alphabet took little more than an hour to learn, a few more hours to master, and slowly, Mother learned to have whole conversations on her palm. There was medication for the depression.

By the time we moved from the North York townhouse that had always been our home to the suburban bungalow in Markham that never felt like home, two of us had grown up enough to go off elsewhere. One of us moved away Labour Day weekend to begin a degree in Microbiology and another of us moved away unannounced in the middle of the night, not to be heard from in nearly a year. We saw nothing odd in this discrepancy. We had skipped our grade eight and grade thirteen graduation ceremonies. We had begun shoplifting. We had stopped our habit of falling into meaningless crushes and committed instead to schoolwork. We had kissed the married woman on our paper route whose breath smelled of alcohol.

The new house sat east of the city, and its single floor was a preemptive measure against the wheelchair that would come.

Every light switch was waist height and the kitchen wallphone was mounted at the same level as the linoleum countertop. The main and the ensuite baths were equipped with support grips and grab bars anchored to the walls around the toilet and tub, and a wooden ramp covered the three steps out of the back and side patio doors. All of these accommodations had been made by the previous owners, a single father and his teenaged girl, a thirteen year-old with muscular dystrophy. Since real estate brokers handled the listing, we never saw the father and daughter, but sometimes we pictured them, and in our imagination, the poor young girl was pretty with red hair and the father looked very much like our own father. Tired, old.

Because Mother was free from the worst of her symptoms at the time of the move, she threw her limited energy into redecorating and undoing the aesthetic offenses committed by the previous owner. In addition to the wheelchair accommodations, the father had wallpapered a mural of a Venice canal on the living room's long wall, and Mother joked she could not sit on the chesterfield without feeling the gondola driver's lecherous eyes all over her. Once the mural was stripped from the walls and the room repainted in taupe, she moved onto the kitchen, where she refaced the cupboards with a wood finish in a birch stain, and by the end of summer, she was well into her third project—ridding the main hallway of its unfortunate white and powder blue fleur-de-lis wallpaper. On what would have been her second day of stripping the paper, though, she awoke without the strength to stand. Her legs weren't entirely useless—with some effort, she could cross and uncross them—but they would not support her weight. She purchased her first wheelchair, and as predicted, the bungalow was necessary.

With a new school year starting, we were preoccupied, and with his longer commute downtown to work, Father had even less time than usual. It took months to finish the hallway project, and the wallpaper scraps of fleur-de-lis weren't all gone until Christmas break.

With changing symptoms came varying medications, and because her pills and doses were constantly readjusted, Mother's behaviour could be erratic. One evening she set out a dangerously under-cooked pot roast on a bed of mushy peas and hard potatoes.

"You'll have to forgive me," she said. "My mind was elsewhere."

The phrase became a family joke. We used it as a comic excuse when we forgot to retrieve the garbage cans from the end of the driveway. We used it when we dented the fender of the station wagon against the side of the carport. We used it to mock Father when his attention drifted away from the dinner conversation, and God knows what he was worrying about.

"You'll have to excuse me, my mind was elsewhere."

Over time, the phrase's function became more generalized, a non-sequitur muttered in a deadpan voice to excuse life's disappointments both great and small. When Father returned from the mall with an orange dress shirt Mother didn't care for, and they somehow wound up arguing for hours. When we came home with an F in grade 13 Calculus, and we were told our chances at university were slim. When Mother forgot a birthday.

"Now tell me the truth, does this look like it was decorated by a blind woman?"

Another family joke, something Mother said for the first time during a blind Christmas. She had dragged out and assembled our artificial fir one weekday while we were all out of the house, and then she'd set about sightlessly arranging the lights, garlands, and ornaments herself. There was an attempt to space the decorations out, but the whole thing was off, the garland twisted over itself and the blinking lights buried in clumps of tinsel. We laughed and took turns repeating her words every year, and now of course, the phrase comes to mind each and every Christmas season when we trim the tree with our own families.

Christmas also makes us think about a particular set of coloured glass ornaments, a collection of twenty-four bulbs, each one hand-painted with species of bird with detailed plumage and serene faces. A blue jay, a cardinal, and a snow owl. There were more. Held up close, tiny controlled brush strokes were just visible, and we wondered at the patience such fine work demanded. The fragile set shrunk each year, a different bird dropped and shattered each holiday season. When they broke, they made a distinctive splintering sound, and each time she heard it, Mother would let out an exaggerated *whoooops.*

"Somebody's a butterfingers."

After she died and Father became a contemplative widower for a period of years, he talked about those ornaments and how she laughed. They had once been precious to her, he said, purchased during their honeymoon through Scandinavia. Long before we were around, back when she could be funny without being bitter. We cannot remember such a time.

Work. Relapses made keeping a single job difficult, but Mother never did quite give up on the idea, and through the decade and a half of her illness, she managed a patchwork of a career. Whenever the symptoms were manageable or absent for an extended period of time, she updated her resumé, and whenever she met yet another medical professional or yet another charity volunteer, she worked up a network of career connections. The residence manager at BallyCliffe introduced her to the owner of Forest Mills, a small assisted living home in Markham, where Mother worked the evening shift three nights a week for six months. An RN from the March of Dimes introduced her to a school nurse taking maternity leave at Trafalgar Glen, where Mother covered for half a semester. The MediAssist sales rep who brought her walker to the house knew someone at the Scarborough North clinic, where Mother filed patient records and alphabetized insurance information for an entire autumn.

The job she cared for the most and managed to hold onto the longest was her last. At the Addiction Research Foundation, for nearly a year, she oversaw the midnight shift of the youth ward, looking after a revolving door of anywhere between one to two dozen adolescent patients. Because the night shifts reversed her sleep schedule entirely, these young recovering and relapsing substance abusers saw more of her than we did that year. Some of them were there for court-ordered treatment and some of them were there for their third or fourth visit, and although Mother complained that the work was often more baby-sitting than medicine, her concern for them and her delight in them was obvious. She said the ward always had a good number of insomniacs who loitered around the nurse's station chatting for hours on end. They were teenagers, so of course, they'd sometimes complain on about their parents, but not as often you might expect. Mostly, what they talked about was music or movies or books.

"Things that no one but a teenager could be so passionate about."

At the time, those of us still living at home were teenagers, and we might have been justified in resenting these strangers to us, but we did not. We understood that she cared for them as much as she did because they knew nothing of her illness. She cared for them so much because they had never had to care for her.

§

While the frequency and range of symptoms varies from individual to individual, the average patient with Multiple Sclerosis suffers from one attack every one to two years during the initial relapsing and remitting phase. Over time during this stage of the illness, the overall number of attacks can lessen, but the patient's resilience and ability to recover from symptoms decreases significantly. After a ten to thirty year period of relapses and remissions, roughly eighty percent of all patients enter into the secondary progressive stage of the illness. During this stage, patients typically demonstrate a slow increase in disability, with periods of remission growing more and more infrequent.

Because her forty-fifth birthday fell on a Tuesday, Father chose to have Mother's surprise party on the following Saturday rather than the preceding one. More of a surprise that way, he said. The family could even have a red herring dinner celebration the week before to throw her off the scent. We could all go out for a family dinner to the Queenstown Grill, where he could have a bottle of wine and a cake brought to the table and the waiters would chant *Happy, Happy Birthday* when they brought it out. There could be small token presents to mark the occasion, he said, and the real gifts would come the following week. His voice was animated, an animation rare for Father.

The surprise party itself was going to be a Mexican theme. Red and gold streamers, a burro piñata, and tequila drinks from the blender. And finger food was best, he said, taco bites and guacamole dip or some of those spicy jalapeno cheese popper thingies. He'd purchased an LP of mariachi music, which could be playing when we all shouted out our surprises. We were all going to be there, one of us coming home in the middle of a university semester and another coming home for the first time in a long time.

And there would be more than two dozen guests. Zahra from the CNIB. A nursing friend from the Addiction Research Foundation. Through a colleague who still worked at BallyCliffe, Father managed to invite Mrs. Thompson, who, at ninety-three, said she would convince Mother that forty-five was nothing to worry about at all. The slab cake was a chocolate and vanilla marble with the Mexican flag done in green, white, and red icing, and after Mother cut the first piece, Father was going to present her with her real present, airplane tickets and ten days in a beach resort in Acapulco.

He should have known better, we should have reminded him. The shaking started at the Queenstown Grill, a slight tremble that wasn't all that different from what she'd had in the past. She spilled her red wine on the red tablecloth and laughed it off, but when the tremor was conspicuous enough for her to skip work Monday, she went ahead and covered her shifts for the entire whole week. Bed rest was the best, she said. Fatigue only aggravated the effects. Nip the symptoms in the bud. Mother feigned resilience and told us she could celebrate her Tuesday birthday in her housecoat. A well-deserved sojourn from the workaday world. By Wednesday, the tremors were strong enough to throw off her balance and spread all down her right side. The more she focused on staying still, the less control she had of her muscles. Thursday, Father cancelled the surprise party, though he didn't tell her until much later, not until after she'd resigned herself to the symptom, not until after she'd resigned from work.

Once, years later at a family dinner with Father's second wife, the topic of that birthday and the forever postponed trip to Mexico came up over dessert, and Father admitted that he'd purchased full cancellation insurance for the flights and for the beach resort. It turns out he had known better.

§

In time, the tremors slowed, but they would never disappear. Mother still had to put her book on the table in order to read, her handwriting was still illegible, and she was still confined to a wheeled chair for most of the day. Over time, though, she decided that waiting out the symptom passively would never help her return to work, and she considered possible second careers. Work prospects for RNAs weren't good and never would be, but what careers could be managed from a chair? Public Relations? Administration? Accounting? She settled on teaching, knowing that the choice meant filling a few holes in her own education. Her Biology and Chemistry classes from college could be used as transfer credits, as could the few Sociology courses she had, so all she needed to apply for the BEd was a handful of filler liberal arts classes. Classical Studies, Literature, Philosophy, and Psychology. None too taxing. A full time course load and daily schedule were impractical, but if she completed two six-credit night courses every year, she could apply to teaching colleges within three years.

"What else am I doing with my time?"

We thought her plans were unrealistic. We thought her symptoms were too unreliable, we thought her medication and her mind were too unstable. We thought her decision was admirable. We thought school would get her out of the house, we thought education would keep her occupied in body and mind. She neither needed nor cared about our unvoiced opinions. She did, however, need us. With her driver's license long gone, she needed us to drive her to Classical Literature, Literature, Philosophy, and Psychology and with her tremors, she needed us to sit beside her in class to take down notes in Comparative Mythology, Rise of 19th Century American Novel, and Introductory Ethics. Reserved seating for wheelchairs was usually at the very front of the lecture hall, and so, once again, strangers looked at us, sometimes secret glances and sometimes sustained stares.

Mostly, we kept our heads down, and mostly, we robotically transcribed what we heard. Once in a while, though, a professor's words stuck. There was one lesson on learned helplessness in Developmental Psychology that stays with us today. We learned that the learned helplessness experiments were an offshoot of operant conditioning, and we learned that unlike earlier reward and punishment studies to teach specific behaviour, the canine subjects in the learned helplessness study were given repeated electrical shocks which they could neither predict nor escape.

"Over time," the professor said, "the subject animals grew submissive and entirely inactive. They lay in their cages and accepted punishment passively."

To make the night class trips easier, our parents purchased a used campervan with a wheelchair lift. The previous owner had been a paraplegic man who had modified the vehicle with hand controls on the steering column so both the accelerator and the brakes could be operated by levers. As we were not at first used to driving in this manner, our feet moved instinctively to the disconnected pedals, thumping uselessly on the floor, or we mistook the gas for the turn signal and made van pitch violently around corners. In time, we adjusted.

The heavy steel chairlift was another matter. It folded out of the side of the van, requiring nearly two parking spaces, and the motor was loud and slow, raising and lowering our seated Mother on a grated platform that never failed to draw the attention of passersby. She must have realized how she looked on the lift, a shaking crippled queen awaiting her children's assistance to be ferried onto the sidewalk. She was sometimes impatient and she sometimes yelled to be taken off the damn thing.

According to Father, the van's previous owner had been in his fifties, a survivor of some sort of workplace accident, and we sometimes imagined him while we drove to and from night classes. The campervan included a bench sofa that folded out to a bed, a two-burner countertop stove with a bar fridge beneath, and we sometimes imagined that the injured man had quit the world and taken to the open road. He'd just said to hell with everything and took off to see the country. Real life and responsibility had revealed their inadequacies and the man just up and drove off all the way east to Cape Breton, only to turn right around and drive himself all the way west to Victoria.

While we performed any number of care-giving tasks for our mother, decorum spared us the chore of helping her into and out of the bathtub. The responsibility fell to Father, but on her less patient days, we could hear her snap irritably at him as he supported her weight and she reached out for the grab bars anchored to the bathroom walls. Once she was safely in the warm water, Father positioned soaps, shampoos and conditioners within reaching distance before stepping out of the ensuite. This was to give her privacy, but to be cautious, he sat to the side of the door listening for the sounds of splashing water as she lathered and rinsed herself clean. If no noise came from the bathroom, he would from time to time call out and ask if she needed help. The question tended to anger her, and so he most often suppressed his helpless worries. He returned to the bathroom only when called, only after she had pulled the plug and toweled off, only when she needed help getting into her dressing gown.

Thus, he was not present when she first felt the alarming lump under her armpit, and he was not present in the following weeks, when she felt that it had not disappeared but had grown and was growing. A month later, when she told him of the tumour, when he raged and demanded to know why she had not told him of it right away, she was at once bitter and funny.

"You'll have to forgive me," she said. "My mind was elsewhere."

Beginning in the ducts of the breast and extending into the fatty tissue, an infiltrating ductal carcinoma can be addressed by surgical treatments and/or treatments such as chemotherapy and radiation. Treatment options, however, are complicated by the existence of any comorbidity, an existing chronic illness for which a patient may already be taking receiving treatment, including medication or a combination of medications. A patient given avonex for Multiple Sclerosis, for example, will have to cease medication during chemotherapy treatment to avoid potential long-term harm to the liver. Such a polypharmacy can influence the number and severity of side affects and can ultimately change the final outcome of treatment options.

Unlike the townhouse, the bungalow did not have a family room, and unlike years earlier, getting all the children together to announce bad news in carefully considered words was no longer feasible, so we learned through word of mouth. At the kitchen table where we were eating cereal for dinner. In the dorm room where we were writing a research paper we would never finish. On the chesterfield where we were hung over and half watching a sitcom rerun. By the time all five of us learned of the lump, our parents had already seen a series of medical specialists, and a series of treatment options and strategies had already been carefully mapped out: a lumpectomy and initial chemotherapy sessions in hospital for an undetermined period of recuperation and recovery followed by continuing chemical treatments and ongoing monitoring.

"I'll have to put school on hold for the semester," Mother said. "Par for the course, but I'll go back in the summer."

We took her attitude as flippancy, but as it turned out, she was joking not at all. As it turned out, she had already registered and paid for a senior seminar on Joseph Conrad, and as it turned out, she had already gone ahead and purchased *Lord Jim, The Secret Agent,* and *Under Western Eyes* to get a jump on the reading list. She thought she could probably get through much of it during chemotherapy treatments alone.

We stayed in most nights even though our help wasn't always needed. We called home more often even though we had to nothing to talk about. We asked if we could move back home until things settled down even though we knew things would never settle down. We took turns sitting up with her. We made her the milky tea that calmed her stomach. She couldn't concentrate enough to read, so we read Joseph Conrad aloud to her.

After her imperfect lumpectomy and failed chemotherapy, a radical mastectomy was scheduled and Mother was signed into a semiprivate room. The oncology ward provided only two guest chairs per patient, and we took turns visiting, the privacy curtain dividing the room for the illusion of separation but little actual privacy. In truth, voices carried, and it was impossible to pretend that our words didn't reach our Mother's neighbour in the next bed. Conversation was necessarily stiff.

"How are you feeling?" we asked. "You look good. Are you getting sleep? You look like you're sleeping well. Are you eating? You look like you're eating."

After visiting hours, Mother and the other patient slid open the curtain to pass the time, and in theory, sharing their pain should have comforted both of them. In theory, misery should have loved its company, and two cancer patients should have been able to speak openly of their fears. This didn't happen. In her late fifties, Mother's roommate had once been an elementary school teacher and her pointy face bore a striking resemblance to Ms. Seagull, a long forgotten school librarian who'd annoyed our mother to no end. The roommate was married with some mucky muck of a husband, and they had no children. When Mother spoke to us of this, we held a finger to our mouths to settle her down, to remind her that her derisive words could be overheard through the privacy curtain, but as her medication increased more and more, she cared for etiquette less and less.

"And vain? That woman is vain like you wouldn't believe. As if losing a breast was the end of the world. Oh, so sad. Thinks she knows all about suffering, does she?"

After the operation, Mother moved to a private room to recover, and we were allowed to visit in larger groups.

Studies investigating the link between emotional stress and the onset of symptoms have been at once inconclusive and conflicting, but given the unpredictably of recurring symptoms and the unreliability of quantifying emotional reactions, this lack of verifiable evidence is not surprising. What is worth noting is the wealth of anecdotal evidence from physicians treating Multiple Sclerosis patients in all stages of the illness; mental turmoil and emotional instability are often followed by a rapid onset and increasing inundation of symptoms.

By the time Mother was released from hospital and came home for her final few months, we were all living at home more or less fulltime. Those of us with romantic relationships had taken time apart, and those of us with jobs had taken leave. The palliative nurses for Markham Hospice came once a day, and as we always had with visitors to the house, we smiled polite greetings as they crossed the living room into our parent's bedroom and we nodded polite goodbyes as they crossed to leave. We learned none of their names, however, for these two-hour visits were a reprieve, a time when we didn't have to worry if her doses were correctly balanced, a time when we wouldn't have to worry about helping her to the bathroom. We tended to scatter at the nurses' scheduled arrivals, and while they cared for Mother, we walked the neighborhood and tried to read in the park. We sat against the side of the house around back and smoked. We pulled the phone extension into the front hall and called an ex-girlfriend. Without homecare, we were left to inject the morphine into her central line, the two inches of plastic tubing that extended from her stomach. Without homecare, we were left to support her weight on the way to the ensuite washroom, holding her steady as she bent to pull down her incontinence briefs and squat on the toilet. Without homecare, we were left to prepare dietary supplements in the kitchen blender, positioning the straw in her mouth so she could take her liquid meal in bed. She needed more help when she again lost her sight.

Because medication had once again adjusted her nature and because we sat up with her nights, our Mother wound up confiding in us and revealing more than she meant to during her final weeks.

"It's not like pot," she said.

"Sorry?"

She paused unnaturally and repeated herself. None of the many medicines currently easing her pain and facilitating her sleep were like the marijuana she and Father used to bring on their canoeing trips. There was another pause; these were common in her speech now. Her voice trailed off, her attention drifted off, and then all at once, she returned to the present once again. The Overmeyers came along to camp with their tent once or twice, and one time, they'd brought mushrooms, foul tasting but relaxing.

She asked us if we smoked. Some of us did on a regular basis. All of us had at one point or another. Nearly every weekend in grade eleven, after a closing shift at the restaurant here and there, all the time in first-year dorm. But this wasn't something we'd ever expected to discuss with Mother, so we said nothing and let her continue. She said she dropped one of us in the park while she was bending down to pick up sand toys, and she cheated on a chemistry exam in college, and she sometimes shoplifted from the IGA. Whether or not she understood and remembered, we ended up revealing ourselves during these conversations as well. Most of our admissions were harmless enough. Sneaking the car out, skipping school, an affair with an older man. We told her she never tipped enough in restaurants and when she was blind, we sneaked a few dollars extra. She laughed. Other unsaid confessions came to mind. We thought to tell her she should be more patient with Father. We thought to tell her we never wanted to move to the bungalow. We thought to tell her how we'd eavesdropped as she related her difficult birth story to the Overmeyers years earlier and how we carried guilt once we connected that story to her illness.

She stopped talking about going back to school, but some nights, she still asked us to read her Conrad.

From her diminished perspective, Mother saw nothing wrong in asking Father to plan for her death, not considering how the memorial service arrangements and burial details might be troubling for him. For the funeral home, they settled on Markham MacEchnie, and the turnout she estimated at no more than twenty-five to thirty mourners, a guest list similar to her canceled forty-five birthday celebration. The reception afterwards could be held at the house, out in the backyard, weather permitting. Simple catering for the food, and chairs and tables would have to be rented, but without a specific date, such matters were impossible to settle. Father called around anyway, comparing prices and reporting his findings back to her.

When it came to selecting the headstone and coffin, he was relieved to discover that, like the caregiver volunteers and palliative nurses before him, the Markham MacEchnie funeral director would come to the house. In the business of selling such goods and services, he must have been accustomed to meeting with the frail and infirm. He was not, however, accustomed to describing his wide ranging casket inventory to a demanding blind woman, and his tasteful colour catalogues were of little use. High gloss walnut. Mat cherry. Classic champagne. The funeral director read these coffin options aloud. Brass handles, silver-plated handles, wood accent handles and interiors in crepe, velvet, and silk. The objective descriptors might have made Mother grow impatient, but she snickered instead, intentionally highlighting the callous absurdity of the poor man's business.

We saw the catalogues too, of course. Left behind on the coffee table or on a kitchen counter, the thick booklets sat in wait until one of us was caught off guard and flipped idly though the pages. The makes and models had empty arbitrary names. The Trenton. The Heritage. The Fairhaven. Our favourite name was the Pieta. In each photograph, the empty coffin was displayed among generous funereal wreathes and floral arrangements in complementing colours, but without the deceased and attendant mourners, they were still-life tableaus.

In any discussion of a chronic illness like Multiple Sclerosis, the social and familial impact of the condition must be addressed because it may directly affect not only the treatment and management of the illness, but its progression over time. The patient's physical needs and unpredictable emotional health require flexible and understanding partners and family members, and even in the most ideal of situations, relationships between the patient and spouse and between patient and children may become tainted by a sense of hopelessness.

As her condition worsened, the palliative nurses came to the house for longer stretches at a time, and more and more, Father insisted on sending us to off to bed at night. It was simply easier for him to sit up with her himself, he said. What he did not say was that children should not have to care for a mother in such a way. He did not say he wanted to keep us from the wet and soiled bedding. He did not say he wanted to protect us from the worst of her rage and regret. He did not say he wanted to guard us against seeing her ravaged wound of a chest when she tore at her bedclothes. We did not say that a husband should probably not have to care for a wife in such a way either.

Most nights were sleepless anyway. We were alone with a book we weren't reading or we were together staring at a television show we weren't watching. Father shut the bedroom door, sometimes to keep us from eavesdropping on their final arguments and some-times to keep us from hearing the hours she would do nothing but rock back and forth moaning. These sounds traveled through the bungalow nonetheless, dropping off only after her exhausted body fell into sleep. And then, one afternoon, she woke and could not hear, and we realized her final conversations would have to be in the slow tactile finger spelling for the deaf and blind.

As with many of our overlapping memories, it is again difficult for us to pin down an exact chronology, and we do not consistently agree on the order of events that unfolded during our mother's last days. We do, however, all agree that we stopped waiting for Mother's death and started wanting it. She had been confined to a chair before, she had been blind before, and she had been deaf before, but now these losses felt less like symptoms and more like deletions, parts leaving incrementally, and though none of us spoke the words aloud, this was the time when we all said *fuck this noise.*

We overheard many unfortunate conversations in oncology waiting rooms. *It's stage three, but my husband is a fighter. The chemo has wiped her out completely, but she's never given up on anything in her life and she will beat it. He's not going to allow it to control his life.*
Of the many clichés and necessary lies we heard repeated, it was this sentiment that bothered us the most. Did the friends and family members muttering such words to one another actually believe what they were saying or were they merely taking comfort in meaningless words? We chose to believe that the latter, for no one could truly believe the former. Because no one could sincerely believe that optimism and inner fortitude are capable of combating an illness that reproduces and spreads at a cellular level. Because no one could genuinely think that pluck, resilience, and moxie will stop metastasis dead in its tracks. Because no one is naïve enough for such unreasoned reason. No, these sentiments were only palliatives for the friends and family of the patient, and so when we heard them again and again during our Mother's final time in hospital, we said nothing.
Years and decades later, though, we will say something. We will be in a bar in the middle of the day and hear two guys on the stools next to us talking about an uncle with colon cancer. We will be in Tuesday playgroup at the crafts table gluing together a foam daisy with our own child and hear two new mothers gossiping about an absent acquaintance with breast cancer. We will be home alone in our basement apartment and watching a roundtable panel show on PBS and listen to supposedly educated medical professionals as they discuss lung cancer. We will hear these people repeat the popular

cliché about fighting against illness, and losing our composure, we will yell how very bloody wrong they are. Because if the cliché is true, if it is true that inner strength can combat illness, then it follows that the dearly departed and the deceased who succumbed to their illnesses were in some way weak. If we accept that fortitude and character can ward off cancerous growths, we must also accept that the dead somehow lacked the requisite fortitude and character, and this cannot be right. Our mother lasted nearly fifteen years after her first diagnosis, but less than six months after her second.

Once, during her final days, we all found ourselves restless at two or three or four in the morning, and knowing that sleep was unlikely, made our way to the kitchen one by one. Talking was pointless, and we did not talk, but we raised our eyes in greeting to one another. We were sitting at the table with a crossword. We were leaning against the counter and picking the raisins out of an oatmeal cookie. We were standing at the open fridge door and inspecting Tupperware for leftovers. From the bedroom, we heard our father's voice, and without agreeing to do so, we all paused to eavesdrop together as if we were again children and again together at the top of the stairs.

"In and out of rivers, streams of death in life, whose banks were rotting into mud, whose waters thickened with slime, invaded the contorted mangroves, that seemed to writhe at us in the extremity of an impotent despair."

It was Conrad. *Heart of Darkness,* and our father was slowly spelling it out on our mother's hand. We thought she must have asked for the book as a distraction. We thought he must have reached for the book because he had no more to say. We thought that the reading the book was a hopeful gesture no matter whose idea it was. We were glad it was a short book.

ACKNOWLEDGEMENTS

Thanks to my wonderful wife and partner Ke Wei, who read multiple drafts of every story here, and many thanks to my kid Molly, Molly, Molly.

Earlier versions of some of the stories in this collection were previously published: "Laney Wilson and Waiting" in *Grain,* "And to Say Hello" in *Event Magazine,* "Canada Coach 2-21, Montreal to Ottawa" in *Ottawa Magazine,* "Parents of Children" in *The Nashwaak Review,* "The Vasectomy Doctor's Online Presence" in *filling Station,* and "On the April Morning of His Second Ex-Wife's Passing," "Six," "Revenge Plot with Fish," and "Mass Graves" in *The Dalhousie Review.* I am grateful to all the fine and friendly editors of these publications.

Dr. Paul O'Connor's *Multiple Sclerosis, The Facts You Need, Fourth Edition* helped with the information in "Comorbidities" and Russell Banks's "The Guinea Pig Lady" helped with the resolution in "Canada Coach 2-21, Montreal to Ottawa."

This book was written with the assistance of an Emerging Literary Artist grant from the City of Ottawa and a Writers'-Works-in-Progress grant from the Ontario Arts Council. Both grants were wonderfully encouraging, and I feel fortunate to have received them.

 Scott Randall has written two previous short collections, *Last Chance to Renew* and *Character Actor*; his fiction has been broadcast on CBC's *Between the Covers,* shortlisted for the Ottawa Book Award, and twice nominated for the Journey Prize. Randall lives in Ottawa with his wife and daughter and works as an English professor at Algonquin College.